# Who Rides With Vengeance

For ten years, Kirk Brennan had been an outcast from his home territory, unjustly accused of rustling, branded a thief in the eyes of the law and the people of his own town. Now he was headed back, determined that the town, the people, would suffer as he had suffered, and in particular the one man who had falsely accused him.

But when he rode into town, he discovered that people had forgotten him and the crime of which he was accused. His was just another name in the history of the town, vaguely recalled by some, completely unknown to others. Then, in the saloon, Brennan saw the face of the man he had come to kill, the man who had framed him for what he had done himself.

Brennan could have killed him then, could have forced a showdown and beaten this man to the draw. But he wanted the man to know who was killing him – and why!

# Who Rides With Vengeance

## CARL EDDINGS

**A Black Horse Western**

ROBERT HALE · LONDON

ISBN 0 7090 7395 X

Robert Hale Limited
Clerkenwell House
Clerkenwell Green
London EC1R 0HT

Typeset by
Derek Doyle & Associates, Liverpool.
Printed and bound in Great Britain by
Antony Rowe Limited, Wiltshire

# CHAPTER ONE

# THE MAN FROM BITTER CREEK

Kirk Brennan's horse quickened its pace from a lope to an eager gallop as it scented the water in the creek. Overhead, the terrible sunblast of the Wyoming early afternoon was an upended furnace that spewed shimmering waves of heat down on to white alkali and frequent patches of sponge cactus and mesquite, enclosing the desert in a shell of glaring white as it sucked all of the water out of the thin, friable soil, drawing it thirstily into the air, scarcely ever sending any back as rain. This corner of the Double Lance range, where the lush grassland which marked off the northern pastures met up with the more eroded ground that lay on the edge of desert, became a torrent of brownish mud once a year if the rains came, eating into the fertile soil, carrying it downgrade into the desert.

Old Man Herdson had asked Kirk to ride south, to check the fences which marked off the spread from open range land and the Badlands lying close against the southern edge. There had been several steers going a-missing during the past few weeks and it was considered just possible that few, if any, of them had actually strayed. Rustling was rife in this part of the territory and scarcely a season went by without somebody losing a thousand head or more, the best steers and calves, singled out carefully from the main drag, teased up into the low foothills and driven across country to a point where the brands could be changed without interference or unwanted witnesses.

In spite of the crushing, blistering heat, this was a job that fitted in well with Kirk's present mood. He generally preferred to ride alone, to think things out in his mind, the thoughts of a man who rode the long trails.

At the moment, he had more than usual to think about. For some time now, he had been restless, strangely dissatisfied with life, but without knowing why, but gradually it had come to him. He had been a rider for Old Man Herdson for more than two years now. He had seen men who couldn't stay more than a month or so in one place before trailing it out over the hill, others who were more settled in their outlook had bought themselves a piece of land, ploughed it, or put it to grass, building up a herd for themselves, striking out on their own. There was still plenty of land to be had in these parts, land which could be the start of a good, stable life for a man willing to devote the rest of his life to it.

He'd saved enough out of his wages to buy a stretch of land, had had his eye on a piece close to the river. Besides the land, there would be enough over to buy a few head of cattle, not much, but enough for him to get started.

He turned his thoughts to Emmy Herdson, felt a pleasant warmth go through him as he visualised her in his mind; tall, slender as a willow, with chestnut hair that flowed in shining waves down over her shoulders. She had always been there during the years he had worked here, they had been good friends, had often ridden together over the stretching pasture of her father's ranch. But that was as far as things had gone between them. But gradually things had changed. He realised that her feelings towards him were the same as his for her and once or twice he had talked over his plans for buying a piece of the range, starting up his own herd. It would take time, of course, but in a year's time, with a little luck, he ought to have a house built, a corral, a barn and with plenty of water from the river, what more could a man want?

He rode around a humped bend and the creek came into view, glittering like a piece of silver wire in the strong sunlight. Ears back, his mount headed for it quickly, and he slid from the saddle, knelt by the stream, and drank thirstily of the clear, cold water, before washing some of the dust from his face and neck. Flicking the water from his hands, he sat back on his haunches, felt in his shirt pocket and brought out the making of a smoke, rolled the tobacco with deft fingers into the paper. He smiled ironically at the thought that he might be buying himself some of Herdson's cattle to start his ranch. Emmy's father was one of the most powerful and influential cattle men in the territory, hard but fair in his outlook and his dealings with men, but coming down heavily on any he suspected of disloyalty.

Lighting the cigarette, he drew the smoke deeply into his lungs, lifted his head a little, quartering the horizon where it shook behind the dancing heat haze, hard to look at for any length of time, the red glare even penetrating through tightly-closed lids, burning its way into his brain. There was a deep and utter stillness lying over everything and as far as he could see, nothing moved.

Then his gaze caught the faintest movement at the edge of his vision. He turned his head, staring almost directly into the west-falling sun. At first, he was not sure of what he saw. Then he recognised it for a cloud of buzzards, dipping and wheeling in the cloudless heavens, rising and falling in a black cloud. They were a certain sign that death, or something very close to death, lay out there and climbing back into the saddle, he splashed across the creek, rode up the far bank and headed towards the buzzards.

7

Twenty yards beyond the stream, he rode into the dark green brush country. Here was a hell of chaparral, Spanish dagger and junco brush, interspersed with prickly pear, stabbing and catching at his horse's hoofs. It was country through which a man rode at his peril. Those lancing thorns could tear an animal's hide to ribbons before it had travelled fifty yards. A swarm of vicious flies settled about him as he closed in on the buzzards. They lifted in a flock of dark shadows as he rode over a low, razor-backed ridge, harsh, angry sounds coming from their throats. Settling a few yards away, they watched him as he slid from the saddle and moved forward on foot. He moved quietly, pausing from time to time to listen, but there was only the silence and an occasional sound from the waiting buzzards, the scavengers of the desert lands.

It was one of Old Man Herdson's steers. There was no mistaking it. The brand was clearly visible on the hindquarters and there were plenty of tracks in the neighbourhood to indicate that a sizeable herd had moved this way quite recently. Bending, he examined the steer. It had been shot through the head from close range, had dropped and died within seconds. He had seen such a sight as this on one or two occasions in the past, when a lead steer during a stampede had had to be shot down in an attempt to turn the maddened herd. Judging from the tracks which had bitten deeply into the dry earth around the dead steer, the same thing could have happened here, only on a smaller scale.

He did not doubt that this dead animal was just one of a bunch that had been run off the range and driven into the foothills some three miles or so across this salient of the desert. Carefully, he looked about him, searching for other signs. He moved quietly and over his head the buzzards still circled, waiting until he had moved on, when they would settle again. As he moved, he paused from time to time to listen, but all around him the silence was deep and absolute in the green stillness.

Climbing back into the saddle, he followed the trail of the bunch of steers which had been singled out from the main herd. In places, it was difficult where the trail led over hard, open rocky outcrops, but as he worked his way around the swell of the escarpment, he came to rolling and dipping country that lifted and fell in long gradual swells and he was able to give his horse its head as he rode into the low hills which bordered the Herdson ranch. He splashed over another narrow stream, followed the tracks along the bank and up through a narrow gap in the rocks. Heat shimmered off the rocky outcrops on either side of him, throwing punishing waves at him from every side, making breath a labour, turning him edgy and nervous. There was the unmistakable smell of dust hanging in the air and he lifted his neckpiece, reversing it across his nostrils and mouth.

This was new country to him and he moved cautiously, eyes alert. His horse champed at the bit between its teeth, anxious to be moving on towards the far ridge of hills where there was shade, but he held it back. The afternoon sunblast hit him hard on head and shoulders, but the sharp smell of dust at the back of his nostrils, warning him that there had been riders on this trial only a little while before, made him ride slowly. Around a humped bend his mount reared suddenly, almost throwing him from the saddle. He fought the mount down, lifted his lean-hipped body a little in the saddle and peered forward into the heat haze. The horse was standing a hundred yards away on the edge of a wide clearing, but he gave the animal only a cursory glance, his gaze drawn towards the man who lay face-downwards on the hard rock close by, the middle of his body arched a little, his head twisted crazily.

Slipping one of the Colts from its holster, he slid from the saddle and moved forward, went down on one knee and turned the man over. He took in the polished boots, the black velvet jacket and corduroy pants, all smart and well made. This man was no drifter, moving from one camp to another, but the handles of the guns, still in their holsters were smooth with long years of use and the face was hard and pinched with the flesh drawn down tight against the cheek bones and the wide, staring eyes were grey, flecked a little with brown. Kirk's fingers gently touched the other's shirt where the red stain showed the spot where the bullet had smashed into his chest. He certainly hadn't lived long with that slug in him, he decided grimly. But who was he and what was a man like this doing here?

The fact that the other's guns were still reposing in their holsters showed it to be a clear case of a bushwhack. Glancing about him, Kirk's mind sought for a reason for this. There was the possibility that he had somehow got in the way of that bunch of rustlers moving the stolen cattle up into the hills and he had been shot down so that he couldn't talk. There was just the chance that he had been a member of that bunch and had been shot by one of the others, either deliberately or by mischance. Whatever the reason, this would have to be reported to the sheriff.

He straightened slowly, thrust the Colt back into leather, rubbed his chin thoughtfully. His mount snickered a few yards away. Turning, he moved towards it, then stopped sharply as a voice from among the rocks said harshly: 'Just hold it right there, young fella. Don't make any wrong moves towards your guns or it'll be the last thing you do.'

Kirk stiffened, held himself very still. He had recognised the voice instantly as belonging to Matt Culver, the foreman of the Double Lance spread.

A moment later, the other came clambering down from the rocks, glaring at Kirk. There were three other men at his back, one of them with a deputy's star pinned on his shirt.

'It's all right, Culver. You can put that gun away,' Kirk

said sharply. 'It's only me.'

'I reckon I can see who it is.' The other did not lower the gun but kept it pointed at Kirk's chest, his finger hard on the trigger. Without taking his gaze off Kirk, he said to the deputy, 'Better take a look at that *hombre* on the ground, Russ. I figure we're too late to find him alive.'

Culver glanced at the tracks in the thin, sandy soil, his face grim. 'I'd say they was ridden off less than an hour ago.' He glanced briefly up into the sun-glaring hills to the south, reaching out across the blistered wastes of the Badlands. 'What happened here, Brennan? Did you shoot him down so he couldn't testify to the identity of the rustlers?'

'Just what the hell are you talkin' about?' demanded Kirk staring hard at the other. 'If you got any ideas that I might have shot him, then you're wrong.'

One of the other men edged his horse to the far side of the clearing, paused there for a moment, then came back. There was a grim look on his face as he said: 'The tracks lead out yonder where we figured they would go, Matt.' He sidled up to Kirk's horse, lifted the Winchester from the scabbard, sniffed at the barrel, then broke the weapon open and extracted the shells. 'Hasn't been fired recently,' he said significantly.

'Sure it hasn't,' Kirk swung around. 'You seem mighty sure I did this, Culver. Just what have you got on your mind? You know that Old Man Herdson sent me to check the boundary fences here this morning. What are you doin' here?'

'He sent me to check on you,' said the other with a faint sneer on his coarse, heavy-jowled features. 'He's suspected you to be in cahoots with these rustlers for some time now, but we couldn't pin anythin' on you.'

'You're lyin',' snapped Kirk. He moved forward, came up short as the other's finger tightened on the trigger of his gun until the knuckle gleamed white with the pressure he was exerting.

11

'Better watch your tongue, Brennan, or we'll string you up right here for rustlin' and murder.' Culver's eyes were slitted, his body leaning forward a little.

'Like I've been tryin' to tell you,' Kirk said, forcing evenness into his voice, noticing the looks of tight accusation in the eyes of the other men there. 'I found that dead steer back there along the trail, followed the tracks into the rocks and found this *hombre*. I've never seen him before in my life, but it was pretty obvious he's been bushwhacked. I was goin' to tell the sheriff when you appeared on the scene.'

'Sure – sure.' The other's voice was thin with disbelief. 'I reckon you were on your way up into the Badlands to join the rest of that thievin' bunch.'

'You got no proof of that.'

'We don't need more proof than we got,' snarled the other. 'It's talk in town that you're savin' to buy a ranch of your own and that you'll need steers to stock it. Herdson has been missin' steers for a while now. Could be you're building up your own herd this way. But if you're wantin' to see the sheriff, I reckon we can oblige you. You'd better do what you have to, Deputy.'

For a moment, Kirk was at a loss to understand what the other meant. When it did penetrate, it was too late. The deputy had moved up beside him while Culver had been speaking. Now he reached out quickly and plucked the two Colts from their holsters, stepping back and levelling them at Kirk. 'All right,' he said softly. 'On your horse and don't try anythin'. I'm takin' you back into town on a charge of murder and rustlin'.'

'You ain't takin' me anywhere,' Kirk said angrily. He stepped forward, his right arm swinging suddenly. The move took the other completely by surprise, knocked the gun spinning from his hand. Kirk threw a quick, short jab to the foreman's stomach, heard the whoosh of air from the other's lungs, saw the man's teeth gape in agony as he fell back. Then Kirk felt the impact of something hard on the back of his own skull, smashing down on him from behind. He tried to go forward, hands clawing out towards the face of the foreman as the other dragged himself upright but the deputy at his back swung the gun a second time, clubbing him down and Kirk slid to the ground, dropping forward into a deep darkness.

When he came to, Kirk found himself lying across his own saddle, the jolting of his mount sending the blood rushing to his head in a pounding ache. His brain felt empty and numbed, partly because of the blows he had received on the back of his head, and partly from the shock of what had happened. With an effort, he tried to move his arms, then saw through his blurred vision that his wrists were tied to the bottom of the saddle. He guessed his ankles were also tied and forced himself to think clearly.

Somebody had framed him with this murder. Culver's story of having followed him because Herdson suspected he was rustling his steers, didn't really ring true. The whole set-up seemed strangely unreal. Yet when he tried to view the situation objectively, the evidence which Culver could bring against him would be damning. Even if his story about Herdson was untrue, and the old rancher testified in his favour, it might not sway a jury. He could see himself walking to the gallows for something he hadn't done and the thought sent a sudden chill through him.

Turning his head a little, blinking against the glare of sunlight reflected from the ground, he saw that they were moving along the curving ridge around the southern perimeter of the Double Lance ranch.

His movement brought a shout from one of the men riding nearby. 'He's come round, Matt,' called the man sharply.

There was a moment's pause, then Culver's voice sounded close at hand. 'So he has. Well, I figure he won't

13

try anythin' like that again if he knows what's good for him. Let him sit upright in the saddle, but tie his hands behind him. He won't get far like that even if he tried to run for it.'

As Kirk Brennan rode between two of the ranch hands, he had the uncomfortable feeling that this went much deeper than a double-cross on the part of somebody who wanted to get rid of him. He rode restlessly for his hands were tied hard against his back, the cord cutting into the flesh of his wrists.

His eyes were burning pinpoints of anger as he focused his gaze on Culver's back. The big foreman knew more about this than he was telling. Speaking through his teeth, he said tightly: 'Why don't we just ride over and have a talk with Herdson, Culver? Seems to me he ought to be able to straighten out this deal mighty quick.'

The raw-boned man swung sharply n the saddle. 'We saw enough back there for the sheriff to bring a charge against you, Brennan. Ain't no point in wastin' any of Herdson's time. What d'you say, Deputy?'

'Guess you're right,' nodded the other. He did not look at Kirk as he spoke. He seemed nervous and uneasy. 'The evidence against you is pretty overwhelming. If you got anythin' to say in your defence, reckon you'll get the chance at your trial.'

'Can't you see that Culver is at the back of all this? He knows more than he's sayin' and—'

Culver brought his mount close, leaned sideways in the saddle and struck Kirk on the side of the face with his tightly-bunched fist. It sent the other reeling, almost knocked him to the ground. Shaking his head in an effort to clear it, Kirk struggled to keep his balance in the saddle. The side of his face burned where the other's knuckles had grazed the flesh.

'Keep your mouth shut,' he rasped angrily, his breathing sighing in and out through his clenched teeth. 'You've done enough rustlin' and killin', Brennan. We

14

can guess what happened back there.'

Kirk noticed the looks on the faces of the other men clustered around him, knew that the web of suspicion had been coiled too tightly around him for anything he could say to make any difference. Maybe he could make Sheriff Cantry see reason. He knew only a little of the lawman but from what he had heard the other was a reasonable and fair-minded man who would not allow himself to be swayed by any evidence of this kind which had been trumped up against him.

Two hours later, Kirk sat on the edge of the bunk in one of the cells at the rear of the sheriff's office, chin cupped in his hands as he stared down at the floor. Now, for the first time, he was able to think clearly. At first, when Culver and the others had taken him by surprise, kneeling beside the body of the dead man among the rocks, his mind had been numbed, making it impossible for him to think properly. Even when they had arrived in Wasatch, to find that Cantry had ridden out an hour earlier with a posse, looking for the rustlers, he had listened to the deputy's slow, ponderous recital of the charge against him with a feeling of unreality. He got up heavily from the bunk, walked over to the small, square window set in the wall of the cell, just above the level of his head, through the bars of which he was able to make out a small patch of late afternoon sky.

Why should Culver want to frame him for rustling and murder? He had scarcely crossed trails with the other all the time he had been working for Old Man Herdson. There was the fact that Culver had tried to court Emmy some time back, but had made no headway with the girl. She had confided to Kirk later that she disliked the streak of cruelty in Culver, his way of believing that he had only to crook his little finger at any girl and she would come a-running. But was the fact that he had made the grade with Emmy where the other had failed sufficient to justify Culver in trying to have him hanged for a murder he had never committed?

He rubbed his forehead with the back of his hand where the sweat was beaded on the skin, then gingerly felt his cheek with the tips of his fingers. There was a streak of blood on the grazed flesh, now dried and encrusted to the skin and it still stung as he touched it. The smouldering anger inside his mind rose up and threatened to overwhelm him. He had heard the angry muttering of the crowd outside the jail when the small group had ridden up and they had seen the body of the man lying across the pommel of Culver's saddle and the big foreman had lost no time in telling the listening men and women that he had been shot down from ambush by Kirk Brennan. Even now, as he stood close to the window, he could hear the yelling in the distance, guessed that Culver was busily plying the troublemakers among the crowd with free drinks inside the nearby saloon, maybe trying to talk them into a lynching before Sheriff Cantry got back with the posse.

Cantry had been the sheriff in Wasatch for more than five years now and he took his job seriously; an honest man, thorough and determined, conscious of the fact that there were the lawless ones in town who would do anything in their power to make him fall in with their wishes so that they might control the law. So far, he had shown no inclination to work hand in glove with them and his personal integrity and courage were still beyond question.

Kirk leaned on the wall near the window, trying to make out what was being shouted in the saloon, but the voices were all blended together so that he could pick out nothing and in the end he gave up the attempt and went back to the low bunk, stretching himself out on it, staring up at the ceiling over his head.

A little later, he heard the outer door open and someone came into the office. There was the murmur of low voices, one of which he recognised as belonging to the deputy. The other was one he could not recognise.

16

Swinging his feet to the floor, he moved to the door, stood with his chest pressed against it. The door at the far end of the corridor opened abruptly, then the sound of footsteps coming closer.

The deputy stood outside the door a moment later, his face creased with lines of worry. 'Those *hombres* over at the saloon are getting mighty het up about you, mister,' he said thickly. 'They seem ready to make trouble.'

'Don't you mean that Culver is all set to get them over here for a lynchin' party?' Kirk said tightly.

'Could be. He's sure over there with 'em,' nodded the other. He looked at Kirk dubiously. 'I ain't goin' to ask you any damn-fool questions, mister, like whether you shot that *hombre* on the trail or not. Reckon you don't have that much time.'

'Where's Sheriff Cantry?' Why ain't he here to stop 'em?'

'Sheriff's out of town hunting down the rest of the rustlers. He left me in charge.'

'Then it's up to you to stop those hotheads from making trouble here. If you reckon you can't do that, then the least you can do is give me a gun and a chance to defend myself. Nobody's proved me guilty of anythin' yet.'

'Wouldn't do no good givin' you a gun if they do decide to step across here and take you,' said the other. He looked unhappy. 'Believe me, mister, this was none of my doin'. I figured just to bring you here and lock you up so's the sheriff could decide what to do with you.'

'I reckon the fact that Culver's goin' to such lengths to get me strung up before I can talk to the sheriff is sufficient proof that he knows I'm innocent,' Kirk said.

'Possible,' admitted the deputy. There was doubt showing in the frowning wrinkles of his forehead. Kirk saw it and began to push his argument still further. 'You can be sure that if Culver knew I was guilty, he wouldn't mind keepin' me here until the sheriff gets back. He knows I can

17

talk a lot to the sheriff and maybe tie him in with these raids on Old Man Herdson's cattle. Funny he didn't want Herdson to know I'd been arrested. Maybe he figured that he'd clear me as soon as he heard about this charge.'

The deputy rubbed his chin. 'Ain't nothin' I can do until the sheriff gets back. If you're tellin' the truth then you got nothin' to worry about. If you ain't then I reckon—'

'You figure I'll still be alive by the time the sheriff gets back?' said Kirk meaningly. 'Those critters in the saloon mean to see to it that I'm swingin' from the end of a riata long before Cantry comes ridin' back into town.'

'Could be they're just havin' a high old time now that they've brought you in,' said the other, half-convincingly. 'Ain't no harm in gettin' a little drunk after you've been out on the trail all day.'

'You ain't even convincin' yourself,' Kirk snapped. He cocked an ear for any fresh sound from outside the cell. There was a sudden outburst of yelling, as if the doors of the saloon had been pushed open and the men inside had spilled out into the street.

'You goin' to leave me in here without a chance to defend myself?'

'There ain't a damned thing I can do about it. Now stay back in there and keep quiet,' snapped the other, backing away from the door. He turned quickly on his heel, ran towards the office. The sound of his footsteps was lost in a sudden blast of gunfire from the street outside.

The shooting was followed by a brief lull during which Kirk heard the deputy moving around in the outer office. Then there came a hammering on the street door. Kirk squinted through the bars down the corridor. Culver's harsh voice yelled: 'Open up, deputy. We've had a meeting and decided we don't aim to wait for Cantry to get back.'

The deputy's quavering voice called back. 'Now hold on out there, Culver. Brennan's my prisoner here and he stays

18

until the sheriff gets back into town. He'll stand his trial and if he's found guilty, they'll hang him.'

'That ain't good enough for us. Could be some of his friends will come ridin' back to bust him outa jail. We don't mean to take that chance. Now open this door before we break it down.'

There came a fresh outburst of yelling from the street. The deputy shouted something but his voice was lost in the barrage of blows on the outer door. A single shot sounded loud above the cries from outside. It must have been aimed at the lock on the door for a moment later, there was the unmistakable sound of men rushing into the outer office, of the deputy shouting ineffectually and then a bunch of men came along the corridor, keys jingling. Culver came up to the door of the cell and glared through at Kirk.

'Keep this murderin' coyote covered, boys,' he ordered the men at his back, 'while I get him out of here.'

The deputy had appeared at the end of the corridor. He shouted harshly. 'You'll have to answer for this, Culver when the sheriff gets back. You're all actin' against the law.'

'No need for you to get so het up,' Culver answered thinly. 'We're just savin' Cantry time and energy. Ain't no sense in bringin' the circuit judge all the way out here just to find this critter guilty' He fitted the key into the lock, pulled the door open and drew his own gun, motioning Kirk outside. 'Let's get this over with,' he said ominously.

'You dirty—' began Kirk.

'Save it, Brennan.' The other's gun jabbed hard into the middle of Kirk's stomach. 'Rustlers get short shrift here in Wasatch.'

'You've got no proof of that,' snapped Kirk, 'and you know it. Otherwise you wouldn't be doin' this. You know I had nothin' to do with the rustlin' or the shootin'. That's why you've got to get me out of the way right now, before I get a chance to talk.'

'Get outside,' snarled the foreman. He walked behind Kirk, thrusting him in the back with the barrel of his gun, forcing him along the corridor. There was a small crowd gathered in the dusty street outside the sheriff's office. A harsh yell went up as he appeared in the doorway with Culver behind him. One of the men at the rear of the crowd, gigged his mount forward, lifted the coiled rope from his saddle horn and held it high in the air above his head.

The crowd parted to let him through. Kirk stood on top of the wooden steps, turned his head a little, eyeing the hard, accusing faces that peered up at him, knowing he would find neither pity nor justice there. Culver and his men had done their work well. All of these men, some of whom he knew personally, now believed that he was part of the gang of rustlers that had been raiding the ranches around the town. These men had also seen the body of that man who had been carried into town over Culver's saddle.

'We're goin' to string this murderin' rustler up, men,' roared Culver. 'Ain't nobody can say we don't have quick justice here in Wasatch.' The crowd roared with harsh laughter. For a moment, Kirk contemplated trying to run for it, along the wooden boardwalk and around the corner of the building. But the moment for decision was gone. There was the blow of a boot in the small of his back, a spine-jarring kick that sent him sprawling down the steps into the dusty street in front of the crowd. The horse ridden by the man with the coiled riata, reared abruptly as he almost fell against it. A hoof crashed into the dust within an inch of his head as he lay in the dirt, pain lancing through the small of his back. Coughing and choking on the dust that filled his mouth and nostrils, he pushed himself upright, rolling away from the horse.

Dimly, he heard Culver's harsh, mocking laugh, as he struggled to his feet, swaying a little in agony. Culver came down the steps towards him, his eyes slitted against the glare of the sunlight.

Before the foreman could say anything, a girl's voice rang out from along the boardwalk. Through blurred vision, Kirk saw Emmy Herdson running along the front of the buildings, holding the skirt of her dress high, her hair flying behind her.

'Kirk!' She tried to step down into the street towards him, but Culver moved forward, caught her arm and held her back.

'I'm sorry about this, Miss Emmy,' he said quickly. 'But we found Brennan on the South pasture. More of your father's steers had been rustled during the night and we went along to see if we could track them into the hills. We found Brennan near the body of one of the men he had shot. Ain't no doubt that he's one of the rustlers. Reckon he and this other hombre must've quarrelled over some-thin' and Brennan shot him in the back.'

'I don't believe you.' Emmy's eyes were shadowed as she turned and looked across at Kirk.

'He's lyin,' Emmy,' Kirk said harshly. 'Sure I found this man on the trail. He'd been shot in the back like Culver says, but I didn't do it. If they'd taken the trouble, they'd have found that none of my guns had been fired. They wouldn't even ride over to the ranch and check with your father. He told me to ride the perimeter fence today. That's all I was doin' when I found this man.'

'Sure,' said Culver grimly. 'We didn't expect you to say anythin' else. But we've got enough evidence against you to string you up and that's what we intend to do.'

Emmy caught at the foreman's arm, her face ashen. 'You can't do that. Even if you do have any evidence against Kirk, you've got to wait for Sheriff Cantry and see that he gets a proper trial. If you go through with this, my father will hunt you down like a killer, I'll see to that.'

Culver smiled thinly, thrust the girl away with a sweep of his arm. 'We all know that you're mighty fond of Brennan, Miss Emmy,' he said meaningly. 'And you'd do anythin' to save him. But a man's been shot in the back and plenty of cattle have been rustled. For all we know, that gang might be ridin' back to free him.' He turned to the men around Kirk. 'Bring him along and let's get this thing finished.'

Two of the men grabbed Kirk by the arms and hustled him forward along the street. Culver followed, walking beside the man with the lariat. Behind him, he heard Emmy cry out once, but her words of protest were lost in the roar of the crowd, anxious for a kill. Kirk looked tautly about him, but there was no way of escape. The men were all about him now, hemming him in, shutting off every avenue.

On the edge of town, Culver paused, motioned to the lone pine that grew beside the trail. The riata went snaking over the lowermost branch, hung down with the noose dangling, swaying a little in the breeze.

'Bring a horse,' Culver yelled loudly.

The watching men parted almost reluctantly for the man who led the horse through on to the trail. Grinning viciously, Culver pointed his six-gun at Kirk's stomach, his finger hard and white on the trigger.

'All right, Brennan,' he muttered through his teeth. 'Step up into the saddle and don't try any tricks or I'll let you have it in the back.'

'That's the way you fight, isn't it, Culver,' Kirk said thinly. 'The only way you know is to shoot a man in the back, as you probably did that *hombre* I discovered on the trail.'

For a moment, he knew that his shot had gone home. He saw the gust of expression that swept over the other's thick-set features, knew in that second that even if Culver had not been the man who had fired that shot, he knew who had. Then Culver's lips widened in a smile. 'Talk like that ain't goin' to get you out of this neckstretchin' party,' he said. 'Now step up into the saddle before I lose my patience.'

Kirk checked the impulse to move forward and smash

22

his clenched fist in the other's grinning face. Slowly, his mind racing, he moved towards the waiting horse, climbed up slowly and stiffly into the saddle. Now was the only chance he might have of getting free; a slender chance at best, but he might be able to ride through the small knot of men in front of him, hit the trail at a run and be out of range before Culver or the others dared risk letting off a shot after him, for fear of hitting any of the other men. Then the mounted man had urged his horse forward and the rough noose was slipped over his neck.

'Tie his hands behind him,' ordered Culver. 'I reckon he might as well have all the trimmings.' His laugh brought an answering roar from the crowd. Staring down at their faces, Kirk felt a sudden sense of disgust. He knew that most of these men considered themselves to be decent citizens of Wasatch, would have been horrified if anyone had accused them point blank of being murderers, yet here they were, openly condoning this act of injustice, waiting for the excitement of seeing him die without even asking themselves the all-important question: Was he guilty or innocent of the charges which Culver had brought against him?

'You got anythin' you want to say before we cut the ground away from under you, Brennan?' said Culver.

Kirk tightened his lips. His level gaze locked with the foreman's and he said through his teeth: 'Some day retribution is goin' to catch up with you for this, Culver. Maybe I won't be around to see it, but I sure know that it's goin' to happen.'

Culver's lips pulled back in a snarl. He made a quick gesture with his left hand. 'Finish it!' he said thickly, nodding to the rider beside Kirk.

# CHAPTER TWO

# THE TIME OF THE KILLER

Seated in the saddle, with the middle-down sun hot on his back and shoulders, Kirk Brennan waited tensely for the slap on his mount's flank that would send it plunging forward, jerking him out of the saddle. And in that second, his life would end with that one, quick pull on the noose around his neck. He sucked in a deep breath of air, saw out of the corner of his eye, the rider lifting his left hand to bring it down hard on the horse's rump, knew he had only a handful of seconds left to live.

The man's hand started on its downward swing. In spite of himself, Kirk braced his body for that forward leap, tightening the muscles of his thighs as his legs clung desperately to his mount. The next second, a man's harsh and authoritative voice said sharply:

'All right, hold it right there, all of you!'

Opening his eyes wide, letting his breath go in slow pinches through his nostrils, Kirk turned his head slowly, aware that the man beside him had miraculously stayed his hand, was staring past him with a look of surprise on his slack features.

It was a measure of their concentration on the hanging,

24

that none of the men there had heard the riders approach. The leading man, seated easily in the saddle, held a cocked Winchester pointed at Culver. As he moved, the cloth of his jacket shifted slightly, and Kirk saw the bright sunlight glint off the sheriff's star on his chest.

Licking his lips, Kirk said throatily. 'I'm mighty glad you turned up when you did, Sheriff.'

'Maybe so,' grunted the other. His frosty glare switched to the big foreman. 'Seems to me you're tryin' to take the law into your own hands here, Culver. Just what is happenin' here?'

'We caught this *hombre* beside the body of one of those rustlers he'd shot,' muttered Culver harshly. 'We've suspected him of being in cahoots with 'em for some time. Today, we followed him, heard the single shot and found him on the trail into the hills leadin' out from the Double Lance spread.'

Cantry's eyes bored into Kirk's. 'I seem to recollect seein' you some place,' he said. 'Ain't you one of Herdson's hands?'

Kirk nodded. 'That's right, Sheriff. Herdson told me to ride the south range and check the fences after he'd had more steers driven off a couple of nights ago. I found one of the steers lyin' dead in the mesquite. The trail led up into the hills and I followed it for a while. It was then that I came on this horse and the body of a man in a small hollow. He'd been shot in the back from cover.'

'And you claim that you didn't fire that shot?'

'That's right. Culver here, came up with your deputy and a handful of men. They never figured to check my guns and as for claimin' they heard a shot bein' fired, that's a lie. That man had been dead for some hours when I found him.'

'He's lyin' to save his own neck,' snapped Culver thinly. 'Can't you see that, Cantry?'

'All I can see at the moment is that you've appointed

yourself, judge, jury and executioner here,' muttered the other coldly. 'Now suppose that we all ride on back into town and I'll start askin' a few questions until I get to the bottom of this. If this fella did shoot that rustler in the back, ain't much the law can do about that, unless there's a reward out and we have to pay it to him. As for this charge of bein' in cahoots with this gang of rustlers. That's more serious and if you can prove that, Culver, then he'll stand trial and hang if he's found guilty.'

Culver shrugged but his eyes were murderous as he turned his head slightly and stared at Kirk. 'I still reckon you're wastin' your time, sheriff. We bring in one prisoner and a dead rustler, and you ride the trail with that posse of yours and find nothin'.'

'I'm the law in Wasatch,' the other reminded him heavily. 'And there'll be no lynch-law while I'm totin' this badge.' He motioned to the noose around Kirk's neck. 'Now get that riata off him and untie his hands. He's my prisoner now and I'll see to it that he's brought to trial.'

Back in the tiny cell at the rear of the red-brick building, Kirk lay stretched out on the bunk, staring sightlessly at the ceiling over his head. He had never expected to have any sense of relief at being inside the jail, but it was the only feeling he experienced at the moment. It had been a close thing out there on the edge of town, a moment when he had actually felt the dark wings of Death touch his face. His position was still desperate. He knew that the evidence against him was strong now and Culver would waste no time during the next few days while he was in jail, to dig out more evidence to be used against him. It was also possible that he might get word to the rustlers somewhere in the Badlands and they would see to it that he never lived to testify at his own trial, in spite of everything that Sheriff Cantry could do.

Outside, it was almost dark now. The sun had gone down in a blaze of red which had lit up the interior of the cell with a fiery glow. But this had faded swiftly and now he could just make out a square patch of deep purple set with the first stars of night beyond the window. He had tested the iron bars there but they were all set strongly and firmly in the wall and no amount of tugging on his part would ever loosen them.

He fell to wondering where Emmy was at that moment, whether she had stayed in town after the lynching party had taken him out, or whether she had ridden back to the ranch to warn her father of what had happened. If she had ridden out then there was no way that she could know he was still alive, and she seemed his only hope now, the only one who really believed in his innocence.

The men had left him his tobacco pouch and matches and he twisted up a smoke from the makings, placed it between his lips and lit it, sucking the smoke into his lungs. The flare of the match robbed the cell momentarily of its near darkness. He could hear the sheriff and his deputy talking softly in the outer office, guessed that the connecting door was half open. A moment later, there was a flare of yellow along the corridor as an oil lamp sent a glow of yellow radiance at an angle through the partly open door.

Did Sheriff Cantry believe him? he wondered. Or was the other just as convinced of his guilt as most of the townsfolk seemed to be; and only his determination to see justice done had prevented him from letting Culver go ahead with his necktie party that afternoon?

Getting to his feet, he stared out through the bars of the window. A breeze had sprung up with the darkness and he could hear the faint scraping of balls of dried mesquite and weed as they were bowled along the dusty alley before the wind. A group of riders rode into town, whooping and yelling, their voice drifting to him from the direction of the main street. Then there came the sound of a lone rider heading out of town, followed by the creak of a buckboard as it was driven past the entrance of the alley which ran alongside the building. Funny how one could recognise these sounds even without seeing anything, he pondered, drawing deeply on the cigarette. What was happening out there in town? Was Culver busily making more plans to get rid of him? Had Emmy ridden back to the ranch to tell her father of this? Even if she had, was there anything that he could do beyond testifying that he had indeed sent him out to check the fences of the South pasture? That would only explain why he was there, in that area; not why he had ridden out into the Badlands. He ran his hand over his chin. He'd been over it all again and again since they had brought him back to the jail and each time he thought about it, the evidence they had against him seemed to grow more and more damning and conclusive.

Coldly and dispassionately, he tried to assess what chance he would have in court, trying to defend himself in the face of the tissue of lies which Culver and his cronies could weave around him. There was a filming of cold sweat on his forehead as he dropped the glowing butt of the cigarette on to the earthen floor of the cell and crushed it out under his heel. He didn't want to think about this any longer tonight, all he wanted to do was to lie down and sleep, but it filled his mind to the exclusion of everything else so that no other thoughts could find any place there.

There was the sound of two, maybe three, horses, being ridden slowly and quietly along the main street in the distance. They stopped, as near as he could judge, at the end of the narrow alley. He stiffened, pressed himself close to the wall, straining his ears to pick out the faintest sound outside the window. This could be Culver and some men sneaking up to the side of the jail, so that they might shoot in through the bars. Tightly, he edged as close to the wall to one side of the window as he could. He heard the soft, measured footsteps as they moved along the side of the building, coming closer, wondered whether he ought to yell out to Sheriff Cantry on some pretext. His dilemma was simply that he had no way of telling who it might be out there in the velvet blackness. Sucking in a deep breath, he waited, listening to the faint sounds of the oncoming men. The sounds paused directly outside the grilled window, then a soft voice said in a faint whisper: 'Kirk! Are you in there?'

'Emmy!' For a long moment, he could not believe his ears. 'I'm here,' he whispered back. 'But what are you doin' here? I thought you'd have ridden out of town by now.'

'I saw them bring you back and guessed what had happened. Now listen carefully and don't ask any questions. There isn't much time. Culver is over in the saloon talking things over with a bunch of men. It looks as if they may have some ideas of getting you out of jail tonight and finishing the job they started this afternoon.'

'That's what I figured,' he said tautly.

'We've got to move fast. These bars look quite solid, but we're going to try to pull them out of their sockets. Be ready to climb out as soon as I give the word. There's a horse waiting for you.'

'Where do I ride, Emmy? Back to the ranch?'

'No! That's far too dangerous. That's the first place where they'd come looking. You'll have to ride clear of the territory until this has blown over.'

Kirk was silent for a long moment, turning that idea over in his mind, considering all of the implications of it. He was quiet so long that Emmy said softly: 'Do you understand, Kirk?'

'Yes, I heard you,' he answered slowly. 'But what are you going to do, Emmy? I thought that you and me were—'

'I'll still be here, waiting for you, Kirk, when you come back to Wasatch. Believe me, this is your only chance. They'll kill you if they catch you now.'

'I understand,' he said dully. 'But when I do come back, this whole town is going to pay for this.'

'Try not to carry bitterness with you, Kirk,' Emmy said. 'I know that you didn't shoot that man they brought in.

29

But things do look strange and suspicious right now and you can't blame these people for being carried away by what Culver says. A lot of men have lost cattle to these rustlers. They feel strongly about the whole business.'

'If Culver is so determine to have me hanged, then he must be in on this deal,' Kirk said thoughtfully.

'Perhaps, but you'll never be able to prove it.' Emmy raised her voice a little. 'Now be ready to climb out.'

Kirk stepped back a couple of paces from the wall, caught a glimpse of the girl near the window. A moment later, she was gone and a man was crouched there, snaking a rope around the bars, making it fast. There would be a horse waiting in the middle of the alley, Kirk knew and the rope would be fastened to the saddle horn and then the animal would use its strength to tear the bars from the window. If it worked – and it was his only chance – the sound would undoubtedly bring Cantry and the deputy running. There would be little time for him to get free and into the saddle. Once he was mounted and running for the edge of town, he would have no other choice but to keep on riding, knowing there would be a posse on his heels within a few minutes, and that within days, wanted notices with his face on them would be posted all through the territory. He would be a hunted man, staying just one jump ahead of the law. And his only chance then would be to return and force Culver into telling the truth. He felt a faint surge of savage anger course through him, then he tensed himself as he saw the rope strain, heard a horse shift its feet somewhere in the alley outside.

In the near distance he heard Cantry's slow, deep tones from the office. Then there was the unmistakable sound of a chair being scraped back as one of the men there got to his feet and moved towards the door leading back to the cells. Kirk's heart jumped hammering into his chest. If one of them should come along to see how he was, right now, it could mean the end of everything. He tried to squint along the corridor and keep an eye on the barred window at the same time. Then the door at the end of the corridor was slammed shut and the sound of voices from the office faded abruptly. With an effort, Kirk forced himself to relax. Sweat lay cold on his forehead and along the muscles of his back and chest.

The rope around the iron bars creaked with the strain that was being applied to it. One of the bars bent suddenly, then a brick came loose. Kirk's breath was harsh in his throat as he watched and waited. Another tug on the lariat and the iron grating moved ponderously, inch by inch, plaster falling on to the floor of the cell. Seconds later, the bars were gone, crashing into the alley below and there was a gaping hole in the wall. Kirk's body was tensed with the potential energy of a coiled spring, the palms of his hands pressed against the door at his back. A moment later, he launched himself forward, across the cell, leaping upwards, arms outstretched his clawing fingers catching at the rough brickwork on the lower edge of the hole. He hung there for a moment, then hauled himself up with a wrenching of arm and shoulder muscles. Hands reached through, caught him under the arms and dragged him the rest of the way. Gasping, he struggled to his feet, looked about him,. Emmy ran forward, motioned him towards the horse that stood waiting at the end of the alley.

'Quickly!' She thrust him forward. Reaching the horse, he paused. The girl thrust a gunbelt into his hands, waited until he had buckled them on, then said urgently, 'Now go, Kirk. Keep riding until you're out of the territory. I'm sure it won't be long before we find out who the real rustlers are and then it ought to be safe for you to come back.'

'You'll wait for me, Emmy?' he asked, his voice hoarse.

She nodded. For a moment, her arms tightened around him, her soft body close to his, the fragrance of her in his nostrils. She kissed him hard on the lips, then pushed him from her as hoarse shouts came from the jail behind them.

He needed no second bidding. Swinging up into the

saddle, he rode out into the main street, pulled on the reins, jerking the horse's head around, crouching low over the animal's neck as he rode for the edge of town. The shouting behind him died in the distance as he gave his horse its head. A solitary shot was fired after him. Then he was out of the town, heading into the night-darkened country, with only the shimmering glow of the starlight around him to light his way.

There was a lessening of the wind out here, but further back its force had been sufficient to whip the dust of the trail up into his face, half-blinding him, filling the air with the sharp, alkaline dust that stung the eyes and burned his flesh. Now he no longer had to ride with his neckpiece over his mouth and nostrils and he was able to pause now and again in the saddle, twist himself around a little, and listen for any sound of pursuit. He did not doubt that it would come. Even if Sheriff Cantry did not come looking for him, Culver would. So long as he was alive, Culver knew that his life was at stake.

It was near five in the morning, with a deep stillness hanging over the flats, when Kirk reached the towering foothills that stretched to the south of the Badlands. All through the night he had ridden south, watching the stars wheel across the deep black vault of the night, constellations lifting in the east and dipping slowly to the west, the yellow sliver of the moon, long past full, rising on his left shortly before dawn flushed the sky with a pale grey-blue. He had pushed the horse as hard as he dared, not once pausing at any of the streams which had cut across his trail. Once, a little after midnight, he had fancied he had heard the sound of hoof-beats drumming at his back, but when he had reined up and turned to listen, cocking his head to catch all of the sounds of the night, there had been nothing. Echoes from the river nearby, he had told himself, then ridden on.

Now he spurred the horse up into the rocks, the echoing hoofbeats a solid clatter that was thrown back from the huge boulders on either side of the trail. He moved upgrade all of the time now, with the narrow trail twisting and turning in front of him, dimly seen in the half light of the early dawn. The stars were just beginning to dim over to the east and the sliver of a moon was a pale yellow scratch against the velvet sky.

He studied the peaks in front of him as he rode, where they lifted, tall and rugged against the skyline. To his right, it was the pure grassy flow of the range with the tough, strong grass stiff-standing. This might be the outlying reaches of the grassland of some big cow-outfit, he thought to himself. But it seemed unlikely they would have men up in these rugged hills. Dead ahead of him, he saw the dark green blanket of the pines on the slopes of the hills, rode towards them. Almost at once, he came on the milk-white creek that tumbled down from the summit several hundred feet above him, the water rushing furiously over the sharp-pointed rocks of the creek-bed. Here, he reined up, slipped from the saddle and gave the horse a chance to drink. He rolled himself a smoke, lit it and sucked the smoke down into his raw mouth. It burned the back of his throat, tasted sharp at the back of his teeth, but it served to lessen the tension that had been riding him ever since he had been busted out of the jail in Wasatch.

Leaving his mount by the creek, he stepped through the trees, came out on to a ledge of ground that overlooked the trail far below where it wound in a series of curves across the wide grasslands. The sun just lay on the horizon now, throwing a red glow over the high, ragged summits of the hills behind him, although most of the deep valley was still in shadow. From here, he commanded a good view of the trail where it reached far back across the plains, to where he had travelled through most of the night. It looked to be entirely empty, yet a few moments later, as he was on the point of heading back into the trees, he spotted the hazy dust-cloud that lay far to the north. Warned by it, he remained crouched among the trees, resting his back against the wide trunk of one of the tall pines. Nearer at hand, the trail was a grey, mottled snake lying twisted across the land. Gradually, the dust cloud resolved itself into a tightly-knit bunch of men riding hard. Kirk studied them gravely for some time, guessing that it was probably Cantry and his posse hard on his trail. Culver could have joined up with Cantry on this occasion, hoping to be in at the kill and make certain, by any means that presented itself, that he died. It would not be to Culver's advantage for him to be taken alive, and brought back to Wasatch as a prisoner again.

Gently, he eased the Colts from their holsters, checked the guns. They were both loaded with all of the chambers filled. He moved them in his hands, liking the feel of them, their near-perfect balance. He had noticed too, that a Winchester had been placed in the rifle scabbard of the saddle. If those men on the trail decided to take the track up into the foothills, he would have to use the longer range of the more accurate rifle.

The riders seemed to move at a snail's pace along the trail but that was only an illusion due to their distance from him. As they came closer, their speed seemed to increase and for the first time, he had the fear that they might scent his dragged-up dust and know that he was just ahead of them, that he had turned off the main trail. He could see now that there were at least a couple of dozen men in the posse, more than enough for Cantry to split his forces once they reached the foothills if he had a mind to. He was the sort of man who left nothing to chance and Kirk could not see him taking all of those men with him along the main trail down below.

But the posse reached the split in the trail and continued ahead for almost a hundred yards before they reined to a halt. From where he lay, Kirk could make out Cantry at the head of the column. A man had ridden up to him from somewhere near the end, was arguing fiercely with

34

him, gesturing with his arm towards the hills. In the first flooding of sunlight that washed over the bottom trail, Kirk saw that it was Culver who was arguing with the lawman, could guess what the other was saying. Cantry, it seemed, wanted to follow the main trail, was perhaps certain that Kirk's first thought would be to get clear of the territory as fast as he could, knowing that Cantry's jurisdiction ended at the boundary with the next state.

Culver, possibly more versed in the ways men had when they were running from the law, reckoned that he had taken the hill trail. Kirk watched closely, saw Culver suddenly wheel his mount angrily, motion to some of the men in the posse, gesturing them to follow him. Kirk saw about half a dozen of the men move out of the main column and follow the foreman as he turned back along the trail and headed for the rocks. Cantry and the others moved on, skirting the hills and heading out across the plains.

It could have been worse, Kirk thought, eyeing the small group of men who had now reached the bottom of the trail and were putting their horses to the upgrade. Moving back into the pines, he reached his own mount, drew the Winchester from the scabbard, eased off the safety catch, went back to where he could see the trail below him and waited. He knew that he had little chance of outrunning these men at the moment. He would have to force them to keep their heads down, send some shots among them to warn them about coming any further. Then if he could walk his horse back a little way, and then mount up, he would have a better lead on them.

The men came up slow, careful. They didn't rush things as Kirk had expected them to. When they passed around an outcrop of rock which hid them from view for several moments, the noise of the horses stopped for a while, although the sound of their voices was continuing so he guessed they had stopped for a breathing spell, maybe trying to guess where he might be hiding out if he had come this way. Culver was too crafty a man not to know that from up here a man could look out and see over nearly the whole twisting length of the trail, could be squatting behind a rifle, drawing a bead on the first man to get within killing range.

The sun was lifting clear of the eastern horizon now and the heat was beginning to pile up over the earth in a faintly shimmering sheet. The party began to move again after a while, edging slowly up the side of the hill. They came into view once more and this time, he noticed that Culver had dropped back a way until he was midway along the column, the men strung out at intervals in single file. Lying behind one of the upthrusting rocks, Kirk pressed the butt of the Winchester hard into his shoulder and squinted along the sights, making a guess as to distance and elevation-drawing a thoughtful bead on the man in the lead. Taking up the slack of the trigger, he waited while the rider's head and shoulders drifted slowly into the notch on the sight. It needed only one shot at that point to start a panic-stricken rearing of the horses, for they were traversing a long stretch of narrow trail that ran alongside a steep drop on the side. Gently, he eased the rifle forward, tightened his finger on the trigger and let a single shot go. He saw the foremost rider jerk in the saddle as the bullet found its mark, saw him clutch at his chest with a kind of stupefied movement, then sway sideways as he fell. His horse reared in sudden alarm, kicked out with its forelegs. The faint screaming neigh reached Kirk a moment later as the animal lost its head, tried desperately to turn and head back. He knew how the rest of the men would react. Trapped on that ledge, unable to move back without running the risk of going over the side, the men fought to keep their mounts still, knowing that the first wrong move would send them all over the side.

Culver yelled sharply at the men in front of him as two of them began backing their horses away from the frightened animal at the front of the column. The man who had been shot now lay crumpled against the rocky wall that ran along the other side of the narrow ledge. The two riders fought desperately to control their plunging mounts. Almost, they succeeded. Then one man went over the edge, his mount losing its footing on the treacherous ground. The horse went over the side, stiff-legged, the rider screaming full-voice as he tilted in his saddle. Horse and rider vanished from Kirk's sight and a second later, the other man fell too, shrieking at the top of his voice. Sickened a little, Kirk put his gun back into the scabbard. He could hear Culver shouting orders as he tried to make his men keep their heads.

They would be occupied for some time down there, Kirk thought as he moved back to where he had left his horse. Swinging up into the saddle, he walked the animal along the trail for a couple of hundred yards, then touched rowels to its flanks and sent it running forward among the boulders that lay strewn on either side of the trail.

The morning was well gone by the time he rode through a wide pass to the summit and took the trail which went over and down the other side. It was almost noon and the usually fierce sun seemed less fiery on this particular day. As he rode, Kirk squinted up at it, eyeing it curiously. There seemed to be a dulling haze in the heavens now, a kind of blurred dimness that shut out some of the terrible heat of the sun and brought, in its place, a humid stickiness that was almost more than he could bear. His clothing clung to him as all of the moisture in his body seemed to rush to the surface to squeeze itself out through the pores of his skin.

It was not yet full summer here and he had been in this territory long enough to know that this dulling of the normally clear atmosphere meant that a storm was on its way, that soon the sky would cloud over as the thunderheads lifted on the distant horizons and tons of water would cascade from the heavens on to the parched, arid ground below.

The next morning found him far from the hills in new

territory. He felt reasonably certain that he had thrown off any pursuit and although he had stayed awake most of the night, sleeping and eating cold for he dared not light a fire so close to the trail, he had heard nothing to put him on his guard and now, out in the open, with the country flat around him, he would have spotted any pursuit for several miles in any direction. There were a thousand places for a man to lose himself out here, he thought as he rode; small ranches employing maybe half a dozen men, with no questions asked. So long as a man remained loyal to the ranch boss, he had little to fear from the law. Somehow, he doubted if the reward money offered for him, dead or alive, would be enough to bring the bounty hunters after him. If it did, then he would have to take care of them by the only means he had. The sixgun.

He smelled smoke in the air once, but he did not turn aside from the trail to seek out the camp from which it came. Shortly after three in the afternoon, he sighted the small ranch on the horizon, noticed the dust which had been dragged up by a herd far off to the east and turned his mount towards the distant house. There were bone-dry creeks here, testifying mutely to the heat and dryness of the past few months but already, there were clouds beginning to build up like smoke on the eastern horizon, clouds that moved swiftly over the heavens. There was a storm moving swiftly with the wind which had sprung up, blowing the dust with him as he rode. He kept his eyes three-quarters lidded against the sun-glare as he rode, letting the horse pick its own gait now, sitting easy in the saddle, both for his own sake and to make things better for the horse.

An hour later, just as the first heavy drops of rain began to fall, the house and barn came into full view and he rode into the small courtyard of hard-beaten earth which fronted the house, standing between it and the small circular corral. There were two men standing on the narrow porch. Both turned to eye him with curious, appraising stares as he halted in front of the door and sat glancing down at them, waiting for the invitation to light.

One man was tall, thin-faced, with a mop of grey hair which curled around his temples, his face the colour of old leather, cracked with wrinkles, the bright blue eyes looking out at Kirk over the high-bridged nose. The other man was shorter, stockier, broad in the shoulder, with a heavily-jowled face and eyes that seemed to be sunk deep in his head. Both wore guns slung low at their hips and he noted the smooth butts protruding from the holsters.

The tall man looked at him and seemed to be speculating on him before speaking for it was several moments before he said casually. 'Better light, mister, get your horse into the corral. Storm's comin' up fast.'

Kirk slid gratefully from the saddle, aware of the short man's stare on his face as he bent to untie the cinch, sliding the saddle off the horse and turning it loose into the corral. He laid the saddle over the wooden rail. Going forward a little, he rolled a cigarette, placed it between his lips and held it there for a few seconds before striking a match and lighting it. His mouth felt dry after the long ride and the smoke caught at the back of his throat. These men were suspicious of him, were both wondering where he was from and what business he had in these parts. That was his first impression of them and he usually went by a quick judgement of men.

'You got business here or just ridin' through?' asked the short man thinly. There was a note of wintry amusement in his voice.

'Steady, Bob,' said the other shortly. 'I'll ask the questions here.'

'Go ahead,' said the other. 'But I wouldn't believe everythin' he tells you. He's got a maverick smell about him, probably runnin' from somethin' that'll catch up with him one day.'

'A man's got a right to speak in his own defence and I

don't aim to have a trial here on my own porch.' The other gestured Kirk inside the house. 'Better get a bite to eat, stranger,' he said, 'then we can talk.'

'Thanks.' Kirk followed the other inside, knowing that the short man was watching every move he made. A moment later, the heavens opened and the rain came down in driving sheets. The sky was dark except when a vicious flash of lightning arced across it, followed almost at once by the savage roar of thunder, echoing across the low hills.

'This your place?' Kirk asked.

The other nodded. 'That's right. Own a couple of thousand head of cattle. My name's Clem Roberts.'

'And the *hombre* outside?' Kirk jerked a thumb in the direction of the porch.

'Bob Caldwell, my foreman. He's always suspicious of everybody who comes ridin' through. Pay no heed to him.'

'So long as he doesn't bother me, I won't.'

The other looked at him sharply, his eyes taking in everything of the man who faced him across the room. Then he nodded, as if satisfied at what he saw. 'I don't ask questions of any man. If he's runnin' from the law, then it's up to the law to find him. Now, I'll get that food for you. You look as if you've travelled some distance, and fast.' There was a meaning at the back of his words, but it was impossible for Kirk to see the look on the other's face for Roberts had turned and was heading into the kitchen adjoining the parlour.

Walking over to the window, Kirk glanced out into the courtyard, now a sea of mud as the rain cascaded from the grey heavens, the heavy drops spouting in the liquid dirt. Caldwell came inside the room a few minutes later, laid a level inquiring glance on Kirk. He said: 'I noticed there ain't no brand on that horse of yours.'

'That's right,' nodded Kirk quickly. 'Ain't no sense in laying a branding iron on as good a piece of horseflesh as that.'

The other inclined his head a little, evidently not satisfied with the answer. Then he said in a half-interested
manner, 'Clem will probably hire you if you're lookin' for
a job. If he does, there's a piece of advice I'd like to give
you. I've seen dozens of men like you come ridin' this way,
men who've taken the trail over the hills, on the run from
their past. Ain't one of 'em stayed here more'n a few
months. Then they get that itch to shake the dust out of
their shoes and ride on. Soon as a new face appears they
run for the nearest hole. I ain't seen your face on any of
the posters yet, but I dare say it'll be around someplace. If
it is, then I'd advise you to ride out now.'

'You got any say in who gets hired here?' Kirk asked.

'Some,' answered the other. 'Clem has the last word.
He's a good man and I don't want to see him take in any
more strays who come ridin' around with their tails up, all
set to hit the trail and dust along when the law shows up.'

'You seem mighty certain the law's on my trail,' Kirk
said harshly.

'Ain't it?' The other's tone was sharp, much more interested now than it had been earlier.

If he was trying to rile Kirk into saying something he
might regret later, he was disappointed. The words didn't
touch Kirk. He knew the type of man who faced him.
Ready for trouble, ready to meet it more than halfway, yet
a little unsure of himself.

Before he could speak, Roberts came back into the
room, set something on the table. He threw a swift glance
from Caldwell to Kirk and back again, then said: 'I must
apologise, mister, for the way things are here, but there's
no woman's touch on the ranch now, since my wife died a
couple of years ago. Have to fend for myself now.'

Kirk nodded. 'Smells good,' he said, smiling tightly.
'Caldwell here was sayin' you might need a hand on the
ranch.'

'If you're lookin' for a job, then I could certainly use

41

you.' His glance fell towards the guns strapped to Kirk's waist. 'I can see that you know how to handle those guns.'

Kirk's eyes narrowed a little. 'You expectin' trouble?' he asked. 'You said that as if anybody who works for you will have to be used to gunplay.'

'He's no good for us, Clem,' said Bob from the other side of the room. 'He's like all of the others, a man on the run, who'll use this as a stoppin' over place until he has to move along again. Somebody's hightailin' it after him, a posse I'd say. If that's the case, how long do you reckon he'll stay?'

Roberts's cold eyes turned on Kirk, his glance prodding the other as he tried to measure him up. 'You're not green,' he said finally, 'and I reckon that you've probably got the same kind of dirty experience like the others.' For a moment, caution held the other back, then he went on: 'The hills are full of men who make their living driving off cattle from the desert ranges. They will destroy us if they get the chance. Like Bob says, I need men who are prepared to fight for me if the need arises. Some have dusted on when I needed them most. I don't want that to happen again.'

'And if there is a posse on my trail? How do you propose to stop them from comin' here to take me back?'

The other shook his head slowly and there was tightness visible around his mouth and eyes. 'What your past is like is no concern of mine. Evil has to be faced by evil at times. Any man who stands by me has nothin' to fear from the law so long as he stays on my land.'

'And you're big enough to keep them off?'

Roberts made a small gesture with his right hand, then indicated the food on the table. 'You're safe here,' he said harshly.

# CHAPTER THREE

# RETURN TO WASATCH

Kirk Brennan rode down from the high hills one shriek-ing, wind-whipped night with the moon swinging low, a yellow sickle close to the horizon, and the bright cold stars showing at intervals in the gaps between the scudding clouds. The rising ridges of rock lay in darkness on either side of him, folded hummocks of black shadow that loomed up against the angry night. Reaching a bend in the trail, he turned down into a narrow canyon that stretched away in front of him like a funnel of midnight, with only the sound of his mount's hoofbeats and the shrill, high-pitched whine of the wind in his ears.

An hour after midnight, the rain came, sheets of it sweeping over the rocks, stinging his eyes, lashing at his face even when he bowed his head and pulled the wide brim of his hat as low as possible on his head. Down before him, he could just make out the dark wash of the valley but the trail which led north to Wasatch was lost in the dark-ness and rain. He scarcely noticed the wetness of his cloth-ing, the damp shirt clinging to his skin, the water that dripped from the brim of his hat. The further he got

towards the foothills, the less was the force of the turbu-
lent wind, but the rail still fell steadily and there was no
shelter from it.

It was now ten years since he had last ridden out of
Wasatch with that sheriff's posse close on his heels. During
that time, he had brooded over his thoughts, had
controlled the desire for vengeance, until the time had
come when he had decided to ride back, to make the town
pay for everything it had done to him, for the injustice, the
false accusations, the branding of him as a rustler and a
murderer. The driving force was still the need to find
Culver, to force a showdown with the big foreman, maybe
to discover if he was the man who had done the actual
killing and been in cahoots with the rustlers. Once he was
able to do that, he promised himself he would kill Culver,
and that the other would know whose finger had pulled
the trigger that sent him blasting into eternity. He bored
steadily on through the darkness, staring straight ahead of
him, his thoughts savage, private things; a man who
wished to be alone. He had no great difficulty in keeping
awake. Like most men used to riding the open spaces of
the range, he could get by on the minimum of sleep and
the night before, he had camped among the low ridges on
the southern edge of the mountain range among the tall
pines and the rest then had been more than adequate.
Now he rode, wide awake in the saddle, turning over in his
mind what might lie ahead of him.

With the brightening, fresh warmth of a new dawn, he
reined up his tired mount beside a narrow stream. The
grey light rolled down in sweeping waves from the mountain's heights, filling the hollows with light, sending the
shadows out of the silent world which lay all about him.

He built himself a fire and squatted beside it, throwing
the dry pine cones and needles on to it so that it burned
bright but without smoke to attract unwelcome attention.
He did not expect anyone to be riding any of the nearby

trails at this early hour of the morning, but he didn't intend to take any unnecessary chances.

Frying up some jerked beef and beans, he chewed thoughtfully on the food, sitting with his back against the trunk of one of the trees, contemplating the countryside around him, forcing back his memory ten years, searching for familiar landmarks which would tell him how distant the town of Wasatch was, how soon he could expect to reach it.

He drank two cups of coffee, then threw the rest over the fire, killing it. Dropping on to his shoulders, he sank back, pulled his hat down over his face as a shield against the glaring sunlight once the sun came up, grateful for the chance of a rest and the opportunity to do a little clear thinking. There were a lot of things he had to sort out in his mind; and a host of things which could have happened back in Wasatch while he had been away. There was always the chance that Cantry was still sheriff there, that he still had that wanted poster with his face on it tucked away in a drawer of his desk and would recognise him on sight, but somehow, Kirk felt a little unsure about that. Ten years could do a lot to change a man's appearance and memory could dim a lot during that time. There were bound to have been other men on the run in town. It had been something of a hell town ten years before and he doubted if it had changed much since then.

Turning slightly on the rough ground as a sharp stone ground into the small of his back, he told himself that if the worst happened, he would not be able to buck the full weight of the law if it were brought against him. All he wanted was a straight, even chance at Culver, nothing more, just to force the other to admit that he had framed him ten years before. He would take nothing less from life. Bitterness welled up inside him, brought a sharp taste to his mouth and his hands clenched themselves into hard fists as his mind rolled over on itself.

He brought his mind back to Emmy Herdson. What had happened to Emmy during these ten years? Just as he had changed somewhat, had she altered too? Had she maybe forgotten him, married someone else thinking that he had ridden out of the territory never to return? He felt a stab of brutal pain at that thought and pushed it out of his mind with a savage effort. He did not even want to think about that.

In spite of his desire to remain awake and think things out, he fell asleep as the harsh light of the sun began to filter through the pines. It was not until it had drifted around the trunk of the nearest tree, the heat and light then falling full on his face, that he woke and knew he had slept for some hours. He pushed himself upright, rolled a smoke, grimaced at the dry taste of the tobacco in his mouth, but finished it because it relaxed his nerves. Then he rose, went back to his horse, bent and tightened the cinch under the animal's belly. Laying his hands over the saddle, he looked out across the tumbled wash of harsh, cruel rocks, then examined his sixguns before sending a swift look up into the cloudless heavens, searching for a clue to the time of the morning. The sun was not quite at its zenith, but already the heat head had begun to pile up, growing in intensity until it lay like a smothering blanket over the surrounding country; and down below him, the dusty trail shivered in the still air and there was a faint, though persistent, shake to everything as if he were looking at details through a thickness of water that was continually in motion.

This was the point in his life where he came to another fork in the trail, he thought incongruously. He could always turn and ride back along the trail he had come, back over the hills, and keep on riding, never setting foot in Wasatch again; or he could go on down this winding trail and seek out his vengeance on the man and the town that had wronged him ten years before.

46

For a moment, just the length perhaps of a solitary heartbeat, he was undecided. Then he thought of Culver and a few moments later, of Emmy Herdson; and knew that he had no choice but to go on.

A wood chit walked upside down along the underside of a nearby branch and there were other vague rustlings in the underbrush close by. He shifted his cartridge belt unconsciously, squinted into the sun for a further moment, then swung up into the saddle, rode out of the clearing, across the rock floor of a deep bowl set among the rising hills, turned a corner in the trail and put the clearing behind him. Once, he thought, there had been a wide river running down the hillside at this point, but it had long since dried up or been diverted from its original course, leaving its old bed set among the towering boulders, rock walls to either side and tiny islands of rock where the river had been. At the first convenient spot, he edged out of this part of the hills, cut down towards the plains below. Soon, it would be high noon out here and the heat would reach its pitch of intensity, soaking into him, dizzying waves striking him from every direction.

Encountering timber and broken ground, he was forced to backtrack once or twice to find a trail through the rough terrain and he made frequent detours to skirt around places where the ridges were broken away by slides of earth. Once, both sound and voices came to him, fading swiftly as he reined up and moved into timber, away from the main trail. When the sound had diminished into the distance, he moved out of the trees, saw the dust cloud where the bunch of riders had moved past him a couple of hundred yards away. They were pushing their mounts, heading quickly along the trail in the direction of Wasatch. Kirk paused for a moment to debate the position.

He was still unsure of what might have happened here during the time he had been away. Cantry might still be

47

sheriff in Wasatch, might still want him, dead or alive, and if he ran foul of a posse, his chances of getting on even terms with Culver could be very small.

Two hours further on, he scented a cooking fire, traced out its growing fragrance only to find that the smoke came from a small timber shack set away from the trail among a cluster of close-knit trees. The gnawing of hunger in the depths of his stomach prompted him towards the place, caution held him back. It was evident from the way in which the cabin had been built way back from the trail, out of sight of prying eyes, that its owner had no wish – and possibly with good reason – to be visited. It was a quick decision, ended almost immediately.

Turning his mount, he headed along the narrow side trail which led up to the door of the cabin, sat his saddle for a moment with his hands clearly in view, resting on the saddle horn, knowing that he was being watched, that he had been seen the moment he had turned off the main trail, and that there was, in all probability, a rifle trained on him at that very moment, with a finger on the trigger ready to send a bullet into him at the first wrong move he made.

'Anybody there?' he called loudly, glancing about him.

For a long moment there was no movement, no indication that the cabin was occupied. Then the door was thrust open and a tall, lean, lantern-jawed man stepped out, the ancient Sharps rifle on Kirk's chest.

'Who are you?' asked the other harshly. The barrel of the gun did not waver in his hands. 'What are you doin' here?'

'Smelled your smoke out on the trail,' said Kirk easily, letting his glance slide over the other. 'Thought you might have a bite to spare. I'll pay for it if—'

'You from Wasatch?' The other's thick, bushy brows were drawn together in a look of suspicion over the grey eyes.

48

'No. I've come over the mountains. I'm ridin' in to Wasatch, but it's a long pull across the hills.'

'Well ... better light and have somethin' to eat. I got plenty here.' The other spoke reluctantly and Kirk guessed that his first impression of the owner of this shack had been the right one. This was a man who had deliberately drawn himself away from the rest of his fellows, a loner who preferred to be left alone. Maybe there was something in his past which had forced him along this empty trail. It might have been that there was one time when he had been neither better nor worse than the next man, but a foolish break had forced him on to the wrong side of the law; and there had been inevitably either things which had pushed him still further and now he was forced to hide out here, unable to join society again. When he died, he would be buried here, buried and forgotten by everyone.

Following the other inside, his glance strayed to the pot of soup bubbling over the fire. It was this which he had smelled out on the trail. It brought a sharp pain into his mouth.

The other pointed to one of the chairs at the low table. 'Nearly ready,' he said thickly. 'There's coffee too.'

The other gave him a keen survey as he ladled the thick soup into a plate and set it down in front of him. 'You on the run from the law?'

Kirk shrugged. It was the natural question to be asked, but had it been so obvious to the other?

'I figured that.' The old man seated himself at the table opposite him. 'You say you've ridden over the mountains. Why're you headed for Wasatch? I'd have reckoned it would be better for you to keep on ridin'.'

'I've got somethin' to settle first. It's been waitin' for ten years.'

'I had that figured out too,' nodded the other. His face was impassive. 'It always seems to be the same. The old

49

ways of violence that never change.'

Kirk paused. 'I'd appreciate a little information.'

'Yes,' said the other. His tone was such that Kirk did not ask any questions at once but held the man's gaze with his own for a long enough period to warn the other that he would know immediately if a lie was told him or if the other deliberately tried to withhold information.

'Sheriff Cantry. Is he still the lawman in Wasatch?'

'Last I heard, he was,' admitted the other.

'You heard of a rancher named Herdson?'

The other's brow creased in sudden thought. 'Herdson?' He pressed his lips together in a tight line. 'Seems I've heard the name someplace.'

'He was maybe the biggest rancher in the territory when I pulled up stakes ten years ago,' Kirk told him, prodding the other's memory.

The other gave him a bright-grey glance. 'I remember. He lost quite a few head of cattle to a rustlin' gang, had to sell out, two, maybe three years back. You realise I don't hear much livin' out here, off the trail.'

'Seems to me you'd hear a lot more bein' here than in town,' Kirk said dryly. He finished his coffee, sat back in his chair and built himself a smoke. The food had acted as a stimulant and there was a restless feel in him, prodding him to action.

'I hear some,' nodded the other pointedly. 'But what's your interest in Herdson? Was he the man who ran you out of the territory?'

Kirk shook his head. 'I worked for him in those days. He was losing cattle even then. There was a foreman called Culver who framed me with a killin' and with being in cahoots with the rustlers. He tried to have me strung up by a lynch mob but Cantry turned up and stopped the neck-tie party.'

'And you bust out of jail and rode out of the territory?'

'That's right.'

The other turned this over in his mind, his unblinking gaze still fixed. 'This man Culver. He's a big man now. He was the *hombre* who bought out Herdson when the rancher was forced to sell out. He's built up the Double Lance spread into somethin' real big now.'

Kirk sat quite still in his chair, the smoke from his cigarette lacing painfully across his eyes but he scarcely noticed it. This was something he had never expected.

'You're sure of this?' he asked finally.

'Of course I'm sure.' The other got to his feet and walked over to the window, staring out into the close-packed trees.

Kirk clenched his teeth tightly and pondered on the situation. It was not a pleasant reflection but now that he paused to consider things, it did not come as a complete surprise. Culver had probably been planning this move seven or eight years before, had started the gang which was plundering the Double Lance herd. Those cattle which had been driven out of the herd and taken up into the hills had probably not been driven further east to the railhead, but had been kept there, in one of the large valleys, out of sight, against the time when Culver would be able to step in and take over the ranch from Herdson. Whether he gave a fair price for what was left or not, would be immaterial. He would own the ranch and the cattle would be brought down again from the hills. By that time, Culver would have seen to it that there was no one around to start asking any awkward questions.

A lot of half-remembered events began to slot themselves into place in his mind as he sat there, with the cigarette burning slowly down between his fingers, brooding over what he had just learned. Presently, he stirred, stubbed out the butt of the cigarette, turned in his chair to face the other.

'What happened to Herdson after he was forced to sell out?'

'Couldn't say.' The man shrugged, studying him again. 'For all I know, he packed up and went out east. He may still be around. I recollect there was some trouble with Cantry. Herdson swore that Culver was working with the rustling gang but there was no proof and Cantry threatened to toss Herdson into jail if he didn't stop tryin' to gun down Culver.'

'I can imagine.' Kirk spoke through his teeth. He had always felt a strong liking for the pernickety old rancher, had felt certain that if he had had the guts to stay in Wasatch until Herdson could have been informed of what had happened, he might have been cleared. Now, for all he knew, both Herdson and Emmy might be thousands of miles away, somewhere back east, and he would never see either of them again. In any case, he wondered with a faint touch of bitterness, would Emmy have waited for him as she had promised, that dark night when she had helped him to escape from the jail? It was a question he could not answer, something he did not want to think about at the moment, for he now felt that whatever score he had to settle with Culver, had been doubled now by what the other had done to Herdson.

He heaved himself heavily to his feet. 'Thanks for the food,' he said harshly. He glanced through the window to where the lowering sun was throwing longer shadows through the trees. 'I reckon I'd better start ridin' on again. I aim to reach Wasatch before nightfall.'

'Better watch where you tread, mister, once you get to town,' said the other in a warning tone. 'If you reckoned it was bad when you pulled out, it's a hundred times worse now. Culver has got hired gunslingers workin' for him.' He searched for his tobacco, made himself a smoke, rolled the thin cigarette reflectively around his lips for a moment, before lighting it. The flame of the match light danced momentarily in his eyes as he sucked the flame into the brown tobacco. 'Every man there is pussyfootin' it around, watchin' every other man, waitin' for somebody to start shootin'. I been into town once or twice, never seen anythin' like it before and I've been through Dodge and Tombstone in their heydays.'

'Why is it like that?'

The other shrugged his shoulders a little. Then he murmured: 'I guess everybody knows how Culver got that land of Herdson's and there are some men in town who don't like it. They probably threw in their hand with Culver when he took over the Double Lance, but they see him now as a threat to themselves, but they ain't quite big enough to stop him if he does make his play soon. Not unless they forget their own personal grudges and join forces. That way, they might be able to swamp him before he can bring in any more gunmen from the south.'

'I guess I'll just stay around there and keep my eyes and ears open,' Kirk said softly. There was no emotion ins his voice.

'Then move slow and easy if you want to stay alive. Sooner or later, if they don't recognise you, you'll be expected to join up with one side or the other. It ain't easy to choose which is best.'

'Could be I won't line myself up with any of 'em. After all, I'm only goin' back to kill one man. Once he's dead, that'll be the finish of it as far as I'm concerned.'

'It's mighty easy to say that now you're here, but once you find yourself in the middle of a range war, it won't be so easy,' said the other pointedly.

Kirk moved to the door, paused in the entrance of the shack. 'For a man who keeps off the trail, you seem to know quite a lot of what goes on around Wasatch,' he said dryly.

The other grinned, sucked deeply on the cigarette. 'If you want to stay alive in these parts, it's always best to know what the others are doin'.'

53

From habit, Kirk Brennan rode through the twilight at a slow pace, eyes alert. Arid dust boiled up from beneath his horse's feet and hung motionless in the air all about him. The suffocating heat had only gradually faded during the last few hours of his ride across the alkali-filtering Badlands and he felt tired and dusty from the long hours he had spent on the trail. Wasatch was just a few miles ahead but it would be dark long before he came within sight of it.

The reds and golds in the west were soon swamped by the black that came sweeping in from the opposite direction. He shifted position in the saddle, easing the burden on his mount as they climbed a steep upgrade, on to a wide bench of flat land which looked down on to the town. The Badlands he had just crossed were more than fifty miles of nothing; waterless and sterile, covered with the white, stinging, alkali dust that itched a man's hide and burned his eyes and skin. Even here, near Wasatch, the land was little better. Only to the north was it really fertile, where the great ranches lay.

He reined his mount as he reached the edge of the bench, peered down into the settling darkness over the town. In this neck of the territory, even the towns were harsh and ugly and the night could do little to soften this. The road ran straight as a die through the middle of the buildings which thrust themselves up on either side of it, squat and grim. Yellow lights were showing in some of the buildings. Even over a gap of ten years, he was able to pick out the sheriff's office and close beside it one of the saloons, with light streaming over the top of the batwing doors, out into the street, touching the shapes of men as they walked past on the boardwalk. He turned his head a little, shielded his face with his hands as he lit a cigarette, drew the smoke deeply into his lungs. There was a rising tenseness in him as he sat there, looking down upon the housetops of the town. A couple of horses stood sway-backed in front of the hotel and he could just make out the shape of an old man seated in a high-backed chair in front of the block.

Finally satisfied with what he saw, he put his mount to the rocky downgrade, wiping the grey film of dust from his face and eyes. He smiled without mirth in himself as he rode into the main street of Wasatch and there was no feeling of homecoming in his mind. He felt tired, tarnished and haunted, but this was the price a man paid for having to live as he had over the past ten years. In the ghostly light which filtered from the windows of the houses along each side of the street, he let his mount walk at its own tired pace, his eyes switching from one side of the street to the other, watchful for any sudden movement there which might warn him of danger.

He doubted if any of the ordinary townsfolk would recognise him after all this time. A man changed a lot over such a period and time had not dealt too kindly with him. The firm lines of his mouth were hardened into a cynical look and the need for revenge was stamped on his features. He tried to think of Emmy Herdson as he had last seen her, when she had promised she would wait for him, but the image faded swiftly in the rush of bitter anger as he recalled what the old man in the wood had told him of Culver.

Behind him, out in the direction of the Badlands, a forked tongue of lightning splashed across the heavens. Clouds had swept up from the southern horizon without him noticing it and in the steel-grey moment of the lightning flash, he made out the whole of the town spread out in front of him, the silent horses standing before the long hitching rails in front of saloons and the hotel, the handful of men lounging on the boardwalks, feeling the stillness and the sudden coolness that came just before a storm swept over the country. Turning his mount as he drew level with the hotel, he reined up in front of the two-storied building, stepped down from the saddle, tied the bridle to the rail and went inside.

The sleepy clerk behind the desk threw him a startled glance as he walked across the small lobby. The man was a stranger to Kirk and he eyed the tall rangy cowboy with a deep interest as the other signed the register. Handing over the keys, the clerk glanced at the name written in the register, but there was no look of recognition on his face and Kirk felt a faint relief as he climbed the creaking stairs to the upper floor, walked slowly along the corridor to the room at the very end. It was sparsely furnished, but there was a pitcher of cool water and a bowl on the sideboard near the window. Pouring half of the water into the bowl, he stripped off his jacket and shirt and washed the dust from his face and body. The heat of the day was burned deep into his skin and he felt the sting of it as the dust film cracked and dissolved.

Refreshed, he put on a clean shirt from his saddle roll, then drank his fill from the water in the pitcher. He felt dehydrated, dried out like a warped board left in the hot sun too long.

Fifteen minutes later, he went downstairs, handed the key to the clerk and stepped out into the dark street. Swinging up into the saddle, he made his way to the livery stables in one of the narrow side streets that led off the main street running through the town. He immediately recognised the old man who stepped out of the shadows at the rear of the building. The other squinted up at him from the dimness, eyes bright.

'See that he gets water and food,' Kirk said quietly, handing the reins to the other.

'You've ridden a long way,' observed the other, eyeing the sweat lather on the horse's flanks. 'I'll give him a rub down.'

'Thanks.' Leaning his shoulders against the post, Kirk made a cigarette, thrust it between his lips but did not light it. He wanted information from the groom. In a town this size, the groom at the livery stable and the blacksmith were the two men who saw everything, knew everything that went on if only they could be persuaded to talk.

The man came back a few minutes later, accepted the tobacco pouch that Kirk held out to him. The groom's glance slanted up at him as he struck a match and applied the flame to the end of the cigarette. He had a sly look on his face and a beady wisdom in his eyes.

'Seems to me I've seen your face someplace before, mister,' he said at length. 'You ever been in Wasatch before?' He made a hopeful query, smiling thinly. His features were sweat-shiny.

Kirk nodded. 'I've been out of town for a while now. Just got back today. Seems the place has changed somewhat. When I pulled out, Herdson had the big ranch to the north. Heard he's no longer around.'

'Who told you that?' queried the other.

Kirk shrugged. 'Just heard it mentioned,' he answered.

'Well whoever it was, he's wrong. Herdson's still around, but he ain't the same man.' He shook his head a trifle sadly almost as if the fact had something to do with him too. 'Bein' forced to sell that ranch broke him. Guess he wouldn't have minded so much if it hadn't been for the way things went.'

Kirk Brennan studied the other over a moment of silence, then nodded a little. 'You mean havin' to sell out to Culver, his foreman?'

The groom was briefly silent. A hint of hard irony appeared around his mouth. 'Culver's a big man now. Got more'n ten thousand head on the Double Lance accordin' to what I hear. Ain't nobody really knows where he got that many cattle. Or where he got the money to buy Herdson out.'

Kirk checked an inclination to reveal his own suspicions to the other. He did not know how far this man might be trusted. If Culver was as big a man as they said, he might have ways and means of hearing all that went on in a town of this size. Better to keep a still tongue in his head about that until he knew the lie of the land.

'Maybe he was just plumb lucky,' he said. He hesitated a moment to throw a calculating glance in both directions before pushing out into the street once more. Somewhere from the noise of shouting and yelling in the saloon he passed, he sound of a woman's voice came to him, low and soft. It stayed with him as he walked on to the hotel.

Pausing in front of the desk, he said to the clerk. 'I'd like a bath. Any chance of gettin' one?'

'Sure thing, mister,' the other nodded. 'I'll get one of the swampers to bring in the water and get it heated for you. It'll be ready in fifteen minutes. That all right?'

'That'll suit me fine,' Kirk nodded. 'Call me when it's ready.' He went up to his room and stretched himself out on the low bed, listening to the night sounds of Wasatch that came in through the half open window. The storm was still growling to itself off in the distance, moving more slowly now across the wide rocky bench where he had halted before riding down into town. An occasional crackle of lightning split the heavens in a flash of ice-grey brilliance and the accompanying rumble of thunder was a gigantic voice yelling its wrath at the foaming clouds.

Well, he told himself, as he lay there staring up at the low ceiling over his head, he was here, back in Wasatch, and he knew a lot more than he had that very morning. He knew something which made it necessary for him to change his plans appreciably. He had intended to ride in, hunt down Culver, shoot him down after giving him fair warning. But now, it would have to be done a somewhat different way. Culver was a bigger man than he had expected and if a man rode into town, shot down its most powerful and influential citizen, even in fair fight, it was doubtful if he would ride out again. Culver would have

58

plenty of men at his back and it would not be easy to fight all of them off. Besides, there was still Herdson and Emmy to be taken into account. The news that the erstwhile rancher was still in town had come as a big surprise to him. Whether or not that meant that Emmy was still in Wasatch was a debatable point. But knowing the girl, he did not think she would leave her father just when he needed her most. Herdson would have few friends now and many enemies. The minute he tried to make trouble for Culver, it would mean the end of him. He felt a momentary sense of anger deep within him.

This had begun as an uncomplicated mission. Now it promised to be both long and involved. He might discover that he had ridden into the middle of a range war and that was the last thing he wanted. If it happened, there was no way yet of telling whether Cantry would try to stop it, or whether he would throw in his lot with Culver. The sheriff's position was particularly vulnerable. He was elected here by the powerful cowmen and if he went against Culver, he would lose his job. If he wanted to keep his post as sheriff, he would be inclined to do as he was told. Culver was a very different proposition to Old Man Herdson. He would stand no nonsense from a sheriff who strove to be honest in his application of the law; and there was no doubting that Culver would not easily forgive the sheriff for stepping in and preventing him from stringing up Kirk when he had got that lynching party all heated up and ready for a hanging.

Kirk's thoughts were abruptly scattered by the loud knock on the door. A moment later, the clerk's voice called: 'Your bath's ready, Mister Brennan. Water's plenty hot.'

'Thanks, I'll be right down.'

Going downstairs, he passed through the lobby. A lounging cowhand, his back against the door post eyed him intently from beneath lowered, puzzled brows, his

59

gaze fully on Kirk. When the latter's eyes levelled with him, prodding against the man's stare, his eyes fell away and he stared down at the floor underfoot. Brushing past him, Kirk felt a strange and indefinable warning tremble along his nerves. He probed into his mind for some recognition of the other, but found nothing there. He could not recall having seen the other before – and yet there had been something he hadn't liked. He wondered, as he soaked in the hot water, at his edginess.

He felt warm and relaxed as he entered the dining room a little later and found himself a table. There were few people there that night and most of the tables were unoccupied. He sat with his back to the wall, facing the door so that he could watch everyone who entered or left.

Ordering his meal, he waited for it to come, then ate hungrily. It had been a long day and he had felt the need of something in his stomach to take the edge off the pangs of hunger. He was on the point of finishing his coffee when a man entered the dining room, looked about him for a moment and then let his gaze rest on Kirk with something a little more than casual interest. The other hesitated for a moment, then walked over, stood behind the empty chair opposite Kirk for a second, then said: 'Mind if I sit down and talk with you, Mister?'

'Go ahead and talk,' Kirk said evenly, his mind sharply alert for trouble, his eyes taking in the hard, leanness of the other, the smooth-handled guns in their holsters and the small eyes under beetling brows.

The other pulled back the chair and sat down. 'Sour mash,' he said as the waiter came over.

'Right away, Mister Fleck.' The other hurried off.

'My name's Dan Fleck,' said the other softly. 'I work for Matt Culver, boss of the Double Lance range.'

'So?'

The other's gaze hardened at the tone of the single

word. 'Does the name Culver mean anythin' to you, mister?'

'I've heard somethin' of him,' Kirk admitted. 'But I don't see what he has to do with me.'

'He's lookin' for riders and you look like a range man to me.'

'I've done some ridin',' Kirk said slowly. 'But I'm not lookin' for a job. I've got other business here in Wasatch.'

Fleck considered this in silence for a long moment, seemed to be trying to make up his mind about something. 'Now that's as maybe,' he said at length. 'But it isn't wise to turn down an offer like this without thinking it over first. The pay is plenty good. Sixty a month and all found. That's more'n twenty dollars more than you'd get any place else in the territory.'

Kirk checked his surprise. The other was right, of course. Now why would Culver want to pay wages as high as that unless he was hard up for men? He continued to study the other while he sipped the hot coffee. The waiter came over with Fleck's drink, set it down on the table in front of him, then moved swiftly away. There was something about Fleck which Kirk did not like. He was sure of himself, too sure; and dangerous too. Kirk thought he recognised the type. A gunman, first and foremost, ready to back up his arguments with the sixgun if necessary, inclined to meet trouble halfway, hungering for it. Pretty soon, if he didn't get his way, he could turn nasty. Kirk reckoned there might be another reason for these high wages, for Culver sending his men out to look for riders for the Double Lance. He would want to have all of the men in town lined up one way or the other, so that he knew who were his friends and who his enemies. He would not like a man who was in the middle, not on one side or the other, because he would never know which way that man might jump. Offering these high wages too, would entice men away from the other ranches and make it easier for him to move in whenever he saw his chance.

'I'm still not interested, Mister Fleck,' he said quietly, setting down his cup. 'As soon as I've finished my business in Wasatch, I'll be ridin' on.'

'Better think it over real good,' snapped the other harshly. 'Or get your business finished tomorrow and be out of town by sundown. Guess you've got that choice.'

Kirk locked his gaze with the other, said softly, very softly: 'Let me give you some real good advice, Fleck. Don't threaten me, I don't take too kindly to it.'

Fleck gave these words a prolonged study. There was a look on his face which was difficult to define. At last he got to his feet, scraping back the chair. He said thinly. 'Be out of Wasatch before sundown tomorrow. It won't be healthy for you here if you're not.'

Kirk smiled. 'Trouble and me are no strangers. I figure I'll stick around and see how things pan out.'

Fleck seemed on the point of saying something more, his eyes narrowed to stony slits. Then he shrugged as if the matter were closed, turned sharply on his heel and walked out of the room without a backward glance. Kirk sat back at his table. A few moments later, when the waiter came over to clear the cups away, he said in a low voice: 'That *hombre*, Fleck. What do you know abut him?'

There was a faint look of surprise on the waiter's face. He paused for a moment, then said through lips that scarcely moved. 'He came here about three years ago. Some say that he made a bad reputation for himself along the Texas border, killing more than ten men. Whether it was in fair fight or not, nobody seems to know, but he's devil-fast with a gun and big trouble. Culver made him his foreman when he took over the Double Lance ranch from Herdson. He's not a cattle man, but I guess that ain't the sort of man Culver needs to boss the sort of men he's got.'

'Thanks,' Kirk nodded. 'That's how I had him figured. But if Culver's bringing in these hired killers, why isn't the law doin' anythin' about it? Where does Cantry stand?'

The other spread his hands in a wide movement. 'Cantry is sheriff in name only in Wasatch,' he explained. 'He takes his orders direct from Matt Culver.'

Kirk nodded his head slowly. Things were beginning to make sense now. It was the same old picture as he had seen happen in half a dozen towns like this. There were few men who could take over the post of sheriff and hold it in the face of the lawless breed, without taking orders from them. Men such as Wyatt Earp and Matt Dillon were few and far between.

He went up to his room, stood at the window, watching the sky in the distance over the tops of the buildings on the far side of the main street. There were still occasional lightning flashes lacing the heavens with a fiery network, but they seemed more distant now and the rumbles of thunder were fainter. The storm had passed by Wasatch and was moving off to the north, only a few saw-edged flicks of lightning flashing downward from the clouds. Down below, in the street, there was still plenty of movement and talk, men on the boardwalks, riders swinging along with the beams of light from the houses reaching out into the shadowed middle of the roadway, touching their faces as they passed through them. He turned over Fleck's threat in his mind as he stood there, watching the riders. Things were happening just a little too quickly for his liking. Soon, Fleck would tell Culver about the presence in town of a man who might cause trouble, and if Culver started asking questions around, he might find out who it was and this would force Kirk's hand.

Allowing his gaze to drift slowly along the dark-shadowed street, he caught a sudden glimpse of furtive movement at the very edge of his vision. At first, he was not able to see clearly what it was; then he saw the man move across a swathe of light. For a brief second, he had a clear view of the other's face and although the man was on the other

63

side of the street, he recognised the other at once. There was a feeling of shock in his mind as the other moved forward again, pausing in the light. The face was lined, eyes deep-sunk, bitterness and despair written there. But he knew at once that this was Emmy's father, the one-time owner of the largest ranch in the territory!

# CHAPTER FOUR

# RANGE LAW

It was near eight in the morning when Kirk woke with sunlight streaming in through the window. Even as he swung his legs to the floor and stood up, he recalled the man he had seen in the beams of light, Emmy's father, a broken shadow of the man he had once known. The previous evening he had been in two minds about following the other, trying to get him to talk, but Herdson had moved quickly along the street and vanished around a dark corner and he had decided he had little chance of finding him that night. Buckling his gunbelt about him, he made his way downstairs, had breakfast in the dining room, then went out into the street. The sun had been up for the best part of an hour and heat was beginning to flood into the town. On the boardwalk, he hesitated, wondering where to begin looking for Herdson and Emmy. It was possible that the groom at the livery stable knew something, but the other might be chary about answering such direct questions from a stranger. He turned to scrutinise the storefronts around him. A few were open and there was also a cafe nearby. He chose one of the stores, made certain there were no customers inside, then stepped through the open doorway.

The man behind the counter was fat, with flabby features that were already covered with perspiration. He mopped at his broad forehead with a red handkerchief, gave Kirk an oily smile.

'Goin' to be hot again today,' he observed.

Kirk nodded. 'That storm last night didn't make it any cooler,' he agreed. He leaned his elbows on the counter, head thrust forward a little. 'I'm lookin' for an old friend of mine,' he said in a confidential tone. 'Used to know him some years back but I haven't been able to locate him now.'

'Could be I can help you, mister,' said the other quietly. 'What's his name? If he's still in town, I might know where he is.'

'He had a big spread north of here in those days. Name of Herdson. Had a pretty daughter too I remember.'

'Herdson?' For a moment Kirk was certain there had been a fleeting look of fear at the back of the other's narrowed eyes, but it was quickly gone and he could not be sure.

'That's right. I know he's still around. I spotted him from my room last night, but I'd no chance to get out into the street and speak to him.'

'You must've been mistaken,' murmured the other. Sweat beaded his forehead. 'Last I heard, he'd pulled out and headed back East. Guess he didn't like it when he had to sell out to Culver. Can't say I blame him. There might have been somethin' funny about that deal, but only Culver knows that and he ain't done any talkin'.'

'You're lyin',' Kirk said sharply. There was no expression on his face. He thrust himself a little further over the counter until his eyes were on a level with the other's and his face only a few inches away. 'If you're worried about Culver findin' out that you've been talkin' to me, forget it. All I want to know is where Herdson is right now.'

'How do you reckon I know that?' demanded the other.

66

He kept throwing swift glances towards the door at Kirk's back as though afraid that Culver or one of his men might walk in at any moment and overheard some of this conversation.

'You're a storekeeper. I figure that Herdson himself, or Emmy, has to come here to buy some food. Besides, this town isn't so big that folk like you don't know what the others are doin'.'

'I—' The other's voice quavered, his glance fell to where Kirk's hand hovered just above the gun in his belt, fingers spread a little, ominously. Then he went on quickly. 'He lives on the outskirts of town. The house stands by itself, a little back from the street on this side. You can't mistake it.'

'Thanks.' Kirk stepped back. 'Now forget that you ever saw me. It'll be a lot healthier that way.'

'Sure, sure.' The other nodded his head quickly, watched him carefully as he moved towards the door, then stepped out on to the boardwalk.

Picking up his mount from the stable, he swung up into the saddle, rode off along the dusty street. As the store-keeper had said, it was easy to recognise the house. It was the only one along that stretch of the main street which did not front right on to the dusty thoroughfare. He reined up and eyed the place carefully for a long moment, aware of the hurried beating of his heart against his ribs. There was no sign of movement behind either of the windows, but he noticed there was smoke spiralling from the chimney and he guessed someone was home.

Slipping from the saddle, he went forward and knocked loudly on the door. There was a pause, then he heard the sound of movement behind it, a latch lifting, and it swung open. He remained wholly motionless for in that same second there came a sharp sound which every gunman recognised at once, the click of a gun being cocked. The unwavering barrel of the sixgun was levelled on his chest, the hand holding the weapon slim but quite firm. He lifted his gaze to the girl's face. She had changed little during the ten years which lay between the moment when he had last seen her and the present. Her eyes were fully on his face with an expression that was changing gradually as if she were fighting inwardly with some memory that refused to return.

'Emmy,' he said softly. 'Don't you know me?'

He saw her eyes widen a little, saw the barrel of the gun in her hand tilt downwards as she lowered it slowly. 'Kirk?' The single word was a question, a faint rising of hope where previously no hope had existed. 'Is it really you?'

He nodded. 'I said I'd come back, Emmy. It's been a long time, but I'm here now and—'

'Come inside quickly.' She caught hold of his arm, pulled him into the house, closed the door and then turned to face him. Her head came right up to his shoulder now and the only difference the years had made to her face were the lines of worry around her eyes and the corners of her full mouth. She smiled a little as she led him into the small parlour, setting the gun down on the table, but there was the suspicion of tears in her eyes when she turned to face him again.

'Father isn't here at the moment, Kirk. But I know he'll be glad to see you. He wanted to help that time when you were arrested. He rode in to see Sheriff Cantry that night, but you were already out of town and there was no way of getting in touch with you. We thought you'd left for good, gone south of the border.'

'I went over the mountains,' he said, lowering himself into one of the high-backed chairs. 'I got a job with a rancher who didn't ask questions and who saw to it that the law didn't intrude on his land. So long as a man worked for him he was safe from the law.'

'Why did you come back?' she asked in a small voice, after a few moments of silence. 'You must have known that

Cantry is still looking for you, that he'll put you in jail if he finds you.'

Kirk leaned forward and caught her hand, holding it tightly in his own. 'I promised I'd come back, Emmy and that I'd clear my name, but there was more to it than that. Culver is the man who framed me with that killing, who had that charge of rustlin' brought against me. I didn't know then why he wanted me out of the way so badly. Now, I think I can understand the reason. He was heading that band of rustlers, taking more of your father's cattle, driving them off into the hills, keeping them there until he could force your father to sell out to him. Then he brought them back from the hills to swell the herd again. Now they tell me that he's the biggest rancher in the territory. His foreman, a gunslinger called Fleck even offered me a job to ride for the Double Lance.'

'They know that you're in town.' There was a note of fear in the girl's voice as she stared at him, wide-eyed. 'Then you're in danger, Kirk. The longer you stay here, the less your chances are. They'll kill you, rather than let you get away. And you can't rely on Sheriff Cantry. He's changed since Culver took over. He takes his orders from him now. There was a time when I thought he was an honest sheriff. Now I know that he's just like the rest, carrying out any orders given to him.'

'That's why I have to stay here. I've got to fight a lot more now than just one man. But I'm determined to make this town remember me, remember the injustice it once did, and Culver is goin' to pay with his life for what he did.'

'Is it worth it?' murmured Emmy softly. 'Getting yourself killed just to try to destroy one man and make the town remember what it did to you? All of this happened more than ten years ago. Most of the people in town have forgotten you. A few of them recall your name, but things have been happening since then, big things, and they won't do anything even if you try to stir them up.'

There was a sudden sound outside and she got hastily to her feet, crossed over to the window and glanced out carefully. 'It's Father,' she said softly.

Two minutes later, the other came into the room. Kirk felt a renewed sense of shock at what he saw. The rancher seemed to have aged thirty years since he had last seen him and all of the fire had gone from his eyes. Broken and defeated, he eyed Kirk through lacklustre eyes and for several moments there was no recognition in them. Then Emmy said: 'It's Kirk Brennan, Father.'

The other hesitated, then nodded. He stretched out his hand in welcome. 'It's been a long time, Kirk,' he said quietly. 'And a lot of things have happened since you rode out. I heard what Culver tried to do to you, settin' that lynchin' mob on you without a trial. I want you to know I never did believe what he said about you, even after you rode out. There were a lot of folk who tried to claim that you must've been guilty or you'd have stayed behind and stood your trial like a man. But I know from what Emmy told me that you had no other choice.'

'Now he's back,' put in Emmy from the kitchen door. 'I'll put on some coffee. I know you two will have a lot to talk about.'

Kirk waited until she had gone into the kitchen, closing the door behind her, then said: 'I've heard a lot of the story from various men in town. It seems that Culver must've been rustlin' your cattle for a long time, herdin' them in some hidden valley in the hills on the borders of the Badlands until he'd reduced your herd nearly to vanishing point.'

Herdson nodded despondently. 'There's no way of proving that, even now,' he said. 'I suspect that the man he accused you of shootin' was a member of the rustlers who threatened to talk. He had to be silenced and my sending you to the south pasture that day provided him with a means of killin' two birds with the one shot.' Sitting back in his chair, the other filled in most of the details of what had occurred while Kirk listened in taut silence. Speaking bluntly, Herdson told him how he had been forced to mortgage the ranch to the bank in Wasatch, how he had discovered too late that it was Culver who ran the bank, who held the mortgage and foreclosed on him when he could not pay on the date.

Kirk listened in a long silence, not lowering his gaze as the other spoke, and when Herdson had finished, he continued quiet for a few moments longer, then said: 'The Double Lance must have a lot of enemies now, judgin' from the hired killers that Culver is bringin' in.'

'It has; mostly the smaller ranches. They fear that he's about to ride in and smash them.'

'Do you reckon he will?'

Herdson shrugged, studying him closely. 'It's possible. He has more than enough men to do it if he can take them over one by one.'

'Then why don't they band together and crush him while they still have the chance?'

'Suspicion. They're afraid of each other. Even if they were to succeed, they're afraid that one ranch might lose more men than the other and be an easy prey to the strongest left in the fight.'

Kirk smiled faintly. 'And the law in Wasatch. I understand that it now belongs to Culver.'

'Not exactly. I know that Cantry is getting old and he's not sure he can stand against Culver. But he does his best to see that everybody gets a fair shake of the dice.'

'In a town like this, that's not enough,' ground Kirk harshly. 'A sheriff has to see that the law is upheld, even if it means goin' against the big outfits and makin' himself mighty unpopular.'

'Culver is ready to back Cantry whenever there's an election for sheriff and as far as Wasatch is concerned, that's enough. So long as it ain't really obvious that Cantry is doin' as Culver says, then most of the townsfolk will vote for him.' A faintly bitter smile twisted the other's lips. 'Trouble too, is that nobody else has shown any inclination to stand for sheriff in opposition to Cantry. It wouldn't exactly be a healthy job if they did.'

'I don't doubt that,' Kirk replied. He went on to tell the other how he had been approached by Fleck, Culver's foreman, to ride for the Double Lance and of the threat to his safety if he refused and stayed in Wasatch after sundown.

Herdson's deep-set eyes kindled with a little of the old fire that Kirk remembered so well. 'What do you intend to do? If you join up with that outfit, sooner or later you and Culver are goin' to meet and although you've changed some in ten years, he'll recognise you at once.'

'I don't aim to join the Double Lance,' Kirk said firmly. He glanced round as the kitchen door opened and Emmy came in with the coffee, setting it on the table in front of them. 'But I do mean to stay here until I've finished my business with Culver.'

'You came back here to kill him, didn't you, Kirk?' said Emmy in a faint whisper.

'That's right,' he nodded. 'I know it won't be easy to get to him now, with that hired army of gunhawks around him but I'm hopin' that so far he doesn't know I'm here.'

'Fleck is likely to talk if you stick around,' said Herdson pointedly.

Kirk looked sideways into the other's face, said gravely. 'I know. That's a chance I'll have to take. I've been thinkin' things over and it seems to me the best thing will be to try to get a job ridin' for one of the other outfits. That way I might be able to keep an eye on Culver without giving myself away.'

Emmy looked at him closely across the table. Her forthright gaze was darker now and unfathomable. She said simply: 'You must be very careful, Kirk. Although he has enemies, Culver has a lot of friends, particularly in Wasatch. You're still a wanted man as far as Sheriff Cantry is concerned and he won't lift a hand to help you if you run into trouble.'

'I'll watch my step.' Finishing his coffee, he scraped back his chair and got to his feet. 'I think I'd better start ridin' before the town comes fully awake.' He turned to Herdson. 'I know how you feel about what happened, sir. Somehow, I've got the feelin' that we can maybe prove how Culver was able to take over your ranch. Once I've been able to tie him in with the rustlin' and the killing of that *hombre* on the trail, it should alter things a little.'

Herdson looked up, nodded his head absently. 'You'll still have to face up to those killers he's brought in from Texas, Kirk, and that ain't going to be easy. There's a bunch of them in town right now. I saw them ridin' in as I came back here. They seemed to be in a mighty hurry, stopped in front of the hotel.'

Kirk's eyes narrowed at that piece of information. He turned it over quickly in his mind. It could mean that Culver already knew who he was and why he was in Wasatch and had decided to take care of him before he had a chance to make any trouble. Not that he would really be afraid of one man; but he was not the sort of hombre to take unnecessary chances when it would be so easy for him to remove any risk permanently.

Emmy came with him along the hall to the outer door. 'Please be careful, Kirk,' she said in a soft murmur. 'These past ten years have been difficult ones for us. Many times my father lost hope, wanted to go back East where he could forget all this, but I persuaded him to stay in the hope that you might come back and help us. Now you're here and I know how you must want to call Culver out and shoot him down. No doubt you're faster with a gun than he is, but he has men everywhere, listening and watching for trouble. Any stranger coming into town is watched all the way.'

'Seems a kind of uneasy town,' said Kirk easily.

'It is. A hell town. A bullet can come out of the night at any moment and kill you. Once they know who you are, they won't rest until you're dead.'

She brushed a vagrant curl from her forehead and their eyes met in a long final look. Watching her, he saw want come into her eyes and without speaking, he caught her around the waist and swayed her towards him, kissing her full on the lips, feeling the blaze of warmth that came out of her, enveloping him. He caught the fragrance of her hair, then pulled back with a sudden movement, saw that her expression had broken, that her eyes were heavy and veiled.

His pulse continued to hammer through his veins as he swung himself into the saddle and rode out of town. A quarter of a mile along the northward trail, he turned and glanced back but there was no sign of any pursuit. If Culver had sent men to the hotel to pick him up, they would know by now that he had somehow slipped through their fingers. Circling an out-thrusting ridge of red sandstone, he rode steadily over the plains which stood on the edge of the wide bench of land in the centre of which squatted Wasatch. Vaguely, he recalled some of the men who had owned the smaller ranches in this territory. Clem Denver, Bob Manson, and several others whose names he could not remember. If Culver was getting prepared to step in and take over their spreads, it might be they would welcome another man handy with a gun to back them against any play that the crew of the Double Lance might make.

An hour's hard riding brought him within sight of the Manson place. He reined up on the brow of a low hill which overlooked the ranch buildings. Clustered on the banks of a narrow river which ran through the spread, they seemed to drowse in the warm late morning sunlight which poured down in almost liquid golden waves over the lush valley.

From his vantage point, he could make out the handful of men in the courtyard and corral, men who glanced up and watched him curiously as he rode down the winding trail which ended in the courtyard. The door of the ranch opened and a man stepped out on to the wide porch, eyed him closely from beneath lowered brows for a moment, than stepped down and came towards him. There was a wary unease in the way the other walked as if expecting trouble. Reaching Kirk's mount, he stared up into the other's face.

'You Bob Manson?' Kirk asked quietly.

'That's my name,' nodded the other. He lowered his gaze for a moment and Kirk noticed a faint look of relief on his face as he said: 'That ain't no Double Lance horse anyway.'

'Should it be?'

Manson's steady gaze brightened; became sharp and appraising. 'We've had trouble with the Double Lance in the past. We've got to be careful.'

'You've been losing cattle recently?'

'We have,' stated Manson. 'Quite a few head. Every ranch has with the exception of the Double Lance. Seems a little more than mere coincidence.'

'Any ideas about it?'

'Sure. I've got plenty of ideas about it, but that's all I've got. I don't have enough men to patrol the whole perimeter of the spread and these rustlers seem to have an uncanny way of knowing just where and when to strike.'

Kirk nodded, bent a long stare on the other, then glanced round towards the men on the rails of the corral. He could see Manson's feelings harden a little towards him as the other debated within himself the reasons why a stranger should ride into his place asking questions like

75

this, but he ignored the other's look as he asked another question.

'I've been talkin' to Herdson who used to own the Double Lance. Seems he got a pretty rough deal when Culver bought him out. He had the same trouble then that you're havin' now.'

'You got any ideas what we should do about it?' There was a note of testiness in the other's tone. 'Seems to me you come here askin' a lot of questions that have nothin' to do with you. Just where do you fit into this situation, mister?'

'Let's say I have somethin' to settle with Culver,' Kirk said softly. 'If I can do it by proving he's a rustler and a murderer, then I mean to do it.'

'I don't doubt that. The question is – how are you goin' to do it?'

In answer, Kirk turned his head, stared up at the small herd of cattle on the higher slopes of one of the hills in the distance. 'It occurred to me that you might have a job for an extra man here. After all, Culver is bringin' in as many men as he can get to back any play he means to make. His foreman even offered me a job at the Double Lance.'

Manson rubbed his chin thoughtfully. 'Why didn't you take it?' he asked tautly. 'He could offer you far more than I can, or any of the other ranchers for that matter.'

'Let's say that this score I have to settle means more to me than a few extra dollars in my pocket.'

Manson stood silent for a while. Eventually he said: 'I think I'm beginning to understand. All right then, stranger; get down and let's clear the air with a little talk inside. You can put your mount into the corral.'

Kirk followed the other into the ranch house. Manson turned as they stood in the parlour, said shrewdly: 'You're not green. I can see that at once. You've had the same rotten experience as most of the drifters who ride through

76

this country with the law on their tail. All stray riders are the same.'

Kirk said equally softly: 'Just what is it that you're afraid of? Matt Culver?'

'Yes,' Manson said. He looked at Kirk with something half formed on his lips. Kirk saw caution hold the other back. His glance was cool and distant. 'I won't hide the fact that I need every man I can get. Ridin' and shootin'; mostly the latter. The men I've got are not enough if there is a showdown. I might have kept the other four men I had a while ago, but there was a raid on the herd. Two of the boys were killed. The others just took to the trail leading over the hill and kept on ridin'.'

'If they ran out of fear and weakness then they were no good for you.'

'It leaves me nearly stripped of men who can handle a gun,' retorted the other harshly. The roughness of Kirk's talk seemed to have surprised him. He walked a slow circle around the room, then stopped near the window. 'I think I know what your interest is in this deal. You want Culver for some reason. It doesn't matter to me what it is, just so long as you don't run like the others did when trouble comes.' He stood square, not looking at Kirk. 'I can see that you're probably lawless and on the jump, brutal too, but if you want the job, then it's yours. There are the usual chores. I've got two crews working the pastures, only a bare handful of men in each though. I'm hopin' to make a drive to the railhead in a couple of months if Culver doesn't start somethin'. I'll get Laredo to take you out to the line camp this evening and you can meet the rest of the boys there. Keep your eyes and ears open when you get there. I'm not saying that I mistrust any of the boys, but information is gettin' out to Culver by some means. He knows exactly where and when to hit the herd. If you can find anythin' while you're there I'll be obliged.

'I'll do my best,' Kirk nodded.

Manson shrugged. It was a movement of his shoulders which said, quite eloquently, that he doubted if the other would discover anything where he had failed in the past, but there was no harm in trying. As Kirk moved towards the door, Manson said slowly. 'By the way, what's your name, mister? Not that it means anythin' to me but—'

'Brennan,' he said, pausing. 'Kirk Brennan.'

The other bit his lower lip for a moment, said: 'Brennan. Seems I've heard that name somewhere before.'

'Could be. It was ten years ago. Culver tried his best to get a lynch mob to string me up from the nearest tree. Claimed I'd killed a man on the trail and been workin' with those rustlers who were runnin' off Old Man Herdson's beef.'

Manson drew his brows together, then his face cleared. The interest in his eyes spread gradually over the rest of his features. 'I recall somethin' of that,' he nodded. 'Funny how you can forget these things after a little while.'

'It isn't easy for me to forget,' Kirk said, his voice hard.

'No, I guess not. I can see now why you want to get even with Culver.' His lips twitched into a parody of a smile. 'Guess I feel a little happier about you bein' out there with the herd, knowing this,' he acknowledged.

Kirk rode leisurely beside Laredo. The latter was a hard-bitten cowhand with a long scar down one side of his face where the needle-tipped horns of a lunging steer had, he said, taken him by surprise when he had been half thrown from his saddle during a stampede many years before. It was a face burned out of life, coloured by the hot sun and savage, biting, dust-laden wind, lined with wrinkles.

They had ridden north-west throughout the long, hot afternoon with the arid dust boiling up beneath the feet of their mounts, hanging motionless about them, a suffocating grey-white mantle which had soon covered them both with a layer of itching, irritating powder. Even after the

78

sun had gone down, the air had retained its heat and the peaks that lay to the north of them still wavered in the shimmering air.

They left the arid plains just as darkness fell, entered the smoother flow of the range itself, riding on the tough, springy grass with their mounts' hoofs making a faint rustling sound as they passed through it. Through the darkness it was just possible to make out where the trail angled around an out-jutting spur of the northward foothills, a fringe of tall trees forming a darker shadow against the hills. Laredo pointed towards the trees.

'The holdin' camp is just on the other side of yonder ridge,' he said quietly. 'We should reach it in an hour or so.' He twisted round in his saddle, squinted up at Kirk. 'How come you joined Manson. Culver will pay twice as much as he can.'

Kirk turned a searching glance on the other. The older man returned it in silence. Kirk pursed his lips and blew out his breath through his teeth. 'I reckon it's because I don't like the way he works. From what I've heard, he's been behind these rustlers from the beginning.'

Laredo lowered his brows. 'You reckon he drove off Herdson's beef, ruined him and then stepped in and took over the ranch when Herdson couldn't meet the payment on that mortgage?'

'I'm sure of it – and I mean to prove it.'

'Won't be easy. He's a cunnin' critter from what I've heard tell of him. Must have been to put one over on Herdson.'

'Everybody makes one mistake and I intend to be around when he makes his. Believe me, it's goin' to be his last.'

The other drew his brows together into a hard line at the tone of Kirk's voice. 'You sound like a hard man,' he observed, chewing on a wad of tobacco which he had twisted from a stick with a wrench of his neck, strong teeth clamped tightly on it. 'But you see how it goes. We've had close on three hundred head driven off in the past four months and never even caught any of the coyotes.'

'So I heard,' Kirk kept his smile as he talked. It was a hard, taut smile; one that held weight and threat and an ominous determination. Glancing about him, he keened the night for any sign of trouble. But there was nothing to be seen. In the east, the moon was rising, round and full, throwing a golden glow over everything, picking out most of the details as bright as day. Ten minutes later, the huge, yellow disc hung directly above a spear-point of black rock that lifted sheer beside the trail, thrusting heavenwards like a pointing, accusing finger, stark and black. Moving through the silent, pleasant night, they heard the faint lowing of cattle in the distance long before they came in sight of the herd, spread out at one end of a long valley. Twin pencils of red campfire were visible against the darkness of the valley. Riding down a smooth slope, they rode up to the nearest fire, the flickering glow lighting their faces as they reined up. There were three men gathered in the camp, with their horses tethered to a rope a few yards distant. The men climbed slowly to their feet as Kirk got down, moving forward with Laredo.

'Jim Coffson, Ed Blaine and Ropey Ellis,' said Laredo, indicating each of the hands in turn. 'This is Kirk Brennan. He joined us this mornin' and he'll be ridin' with us.'

'Howdy,' said Ellis, extending his hand. 'Glad to have somebody new around. We've been expectin' trouble from them pesky rustlers for some nights now and any man who can handle a gun is welcome.'

'You figure they mean to attack soon?' Kirk asked, squatting at the fire, feeling the warmth settle deep in him. There was a pan of beans and bacon sizzling over the flames and a couple of cans of bubbling coffee suspended from a rod nearby.

Coffson shrugged, a big, raw-boned man, with craggy

features that could have been chipped from granite rather than formed of flesh and blood. 'Your guess is as good as ours, Brennan,' he said. 'When they do come, they nearly always take us by surprise even though we are expectin' them. Almost as if they know our movements beforehand.'

'Could be that they do,' Kirk said slowly, accepting the plate that was pushed towards him, sitting with it balanced on his knees as he ate with his bowie knife, chewing hungrily on the food.

Coffson looked up sharply at that, eyes narrowed to slits. The firelight made his face like that of an Indian, his mouth a wide gash. 'Just what is that supposed to mean?'

'Just that there might be someone slipping information to Culver and his men up in the hills,' Kirk said clearly.

'Now hold on there, Brennan,' Blaine spoke up harshly from the other side of the fire. 'You tryin' to say that one of us is givin' that sort of information to them rustlers?'

'Well, it would explain things, wouldn't it?'

The three men were silent at that remark. Kirk noticed how their glances met, then turned as one man towards Laredo. It was Coffson who put their thoughts into words. 'Is this what Manson thinks, Laredo?'

The oldster shrugged. 'I don't pretend to know what Manson thinks, but I reckon there's probably somethin' in what Kirk says. Culver ain't got second sight and the only way he can keep on hittin' us without gettin' caught, is to know beforehand where we are and how strong we are.'

Coffson grunted something under his breath, his voice so low that Kirk was unable to make out the words. But it was obvious that for some reason, the other did not agree with this explanation.

'Can you think of any other way they could know?' Kirk asked pointedly.

The other paused, was silent for a long moment, debating. Then he said thinly: 'Could be coincidence, I reckon.'

'From what I heard from Manson, it's happened too many times to be coincidence.'

'If there is anyone givin' information to the rustlers,' murmured Laredo in a very soft tone, 'then I shall kill him myself.' His gaze moved from one man to the other around the circle of firelight, pausing at each for the barest fraction of a second, then moving on. Kirk eyed the men closely but could tell nothing whatever from their faces.

The moon was lifting towards its zenith when Kirk rode out of the line camp with Laredo, circling the outer limits of the herd which had been bedded down for the night on a low rise of ground where they could be seen from a distance. A dark irregular shadow in the flooding moonlight. Seated easily in the saddle, Kirk let his gaze wander around him. There was a brushy sidehill less than fifty yards from the herd and he was just able to pick out a narrow trail, like a grey scar in the moonlight, running down one side.

Turning in his saddle, Kirk could see the fires blazing high near the stand of pine some three miles distant from this edge of the herd. He felt the muscles draw tight beneath his ribs. To men up there in the foothills, those fires would be clearly visible, would give away the position of the herders. It was just possible that this was how it was done, watching for maybe two hours until they knew exactly how many men were squatting at the campfires, and how many moving in a slow, lazy swing around the herd itself.

He glanced back up to the high ridge, then sucked in a sharp breath, caught his companion tightly by the arm. 'There!' he hissed harshly. 'See him? On the outer ledge.'

Caught in silhouette by the moon, horse and rider were clearly seen for several seconds. Laredo gave a brisk nod. 'I see the critter,' he acknowledged. 'What do you reckon we ought to do. Ride on back and warn the others?'

'He's a sentry, keeping watch on the valley,' Kirk said, 'no doubt about that. It doesn't look to me that we can get a heap closer without being seen. There's a good chance he may have spotted us already.'

'If he has, then why is he staying there where we can see him?' put in the other. 'He'd have ducked back out of sight if that had been the case. I know these mountains. There are nearly a score of crevasses there with half a dozen tracks leading through them. If we skirt around this way, we ought to be able to move up and take 'em from the rear. Reckon it's worth a chance?' He cocked his head on one side, glance bright. 'We can ride along the rim yonder until we can drop down again, come around the end of the ridge and get 'em from that direction.'

'Depends a lot on how many there are,' mused Kirk. 'Two men against a score won't stand much of a chance, no matter how good they are with their sixguns.'

He sat low in the saddle, bending forward over the neck of his mount, his eyes speculatively narrowed.

'Once we opened fire on 'em, it would warn the others and they'd soon come a-riding,' said Laredo. 'Besides, it's the only chance we've had yet of takin' them critters by surprise.'

'All right, let's move.' Kirk felt inwardly uneasy at the prospect of moving in against these men like this, particularly in the flooding moonlight which might be sufficiently bright in the hills to give them away before they could reach within gunshot distance of the rustlers.

There was soon no doubting that Laredo knew this country intimately. He moved from one concealing shadow to another, picking stretches of ground where there was very little moonlight to touch them, and where the grass grew thick enough to muffle the sound of their horses. Kirk rode in his wake, relying on his mount to avoid any obstacles which he could not see himself in the dark shadows which lay across the trail. He did not forego his careful watching of the surrounding terrain, even though Laredo rode with a sure confidence.

A quarter of a mile further on, Laredo set his mount to a steeply descending, twisting drop-off. Halfway along it, the ground seemed to fall away from them in a sheer drop, spread with tumbled boulders. Laredo lifted his hand and waited in silence until Kirk came alongside him, then he leaned sideways and said in a soft, hushed whisper. 'We'd better go on foot from now on. It'd be mighty easy for a horse to put one foot wrong and send stones rattling down this slope to warn the rustlers.'

Kirk hesitated, then nodded, seeing the wisdom of the other's suggestion. He slid quietly from the saddle, hitched the horse to a nearby tree. As he had expected, the footing was perilous and treacherous here. Sharp, needle-shaped rocks lifted from the steep slope at every step and in places, where the tall trees cut off the bright moonlight, there was an inch thick leaf mould which threatened to send them hurtling down the rest of the slope, so that by the time they reached the bottom, Kirk's shirt was damp with sweat, clinging to his body, chafing his flesh with every movement he made. He came to a halt when the other did, crouched down behind a tall boulder as Laredo gestured him to silence. For a long moment, he could hear nothing. Then the faint, unmistakable whinny of a horse came to him, borne on the still night air, from some point less than twenty yards away. He turned his head sharply, staring across at the other.

'We have to be damned careful and quiet from here on,' whispered Laredo through his teeth. In the pale moonlight, the scar on his face stood out starkly and almost obscenely on his flesh, twisting his mouth up a little at the one side. 'Sounds will carry well in this stillness.'

'Where do you figure they are?'

The other motioned him down, lifted his own head slowly, an inch at a time, until he was able to bring his eyes level with the top of the boulder. He remained like that for several seconds, then sank back. His face was a pale blur in the dimness.

'Take a look for yourself,' he murmured.

Kirk lifted himself cautiously. He had an excellent view of the wide clearing just beyond the ring of boulders behind which he and Laredo were crouched. The moonlight flooded into the open space and he was able to make out the shapes of the horses a short distance away, well back near a rim of trees. There were six or seven men in the clearing, most of them indistinct shadows, although one man, with his back to them looked strangely familiar. Kirk felt reasonably certain that it was Fleck, Culver's foreman, but in the dimness, with the moonlight playing tricks with his vision, he could not be absolutely sure of the other's identity.

The sound of onward voices was distinctly audible now. One man, his presence only known by his voice spoke from the moon-thrown shadows near the rim of the clearing where it looked down on to the wide valley which lay spread out below, with the flickering fires of the line camp lighting the dimness.

'They've split their forces, Telfer. Could be they figure they can take us from two sides by doin' that.'

There came a harsh laugh from the clearing and one of the men pushed himself to his feet and walked forward a few paces. This was obviously the man called Telfer. Kirk decided to memorise that name. It was the only clue he had so far as to the identity of any of these men and if he could find that one of Culver's hired gunslingers went by that name, it would give him something to go on.

'Suppose we move down and hit the herd from this side,' suggested another man tightly. 'That way, we ought to be able to steer clear of the fires.'

'They won't be able to stop us once we move in,' was the confident reply from Telfer. His tone had an edge to it. 'I reckon this time, we'll run off the whole herd from this range, take as many of those men with us as we can. You all know what to do. We'll wait for another hour until they're bedded down and then attack.'

Behind the boulder, Kirk lowered his head, bent towards Laredo. 'Did you hear that?' he asked in a low tone.

The other nodded his head. 'We've got to stop 'em.'

'How?' There was a world of meaning in the single word. Kirk kept staring at the one man he could just see from that position, the sentry who had moved out on to a flat outcrop of rock and was keeping a wary, watchful eye on the herd below.

'We could take these men by surprise, probably kill most of them before they knew we were here.'

Kirk drew in a flat breath. 'No, that would be far too risky. They'd drop us for sure before we could get back under fresh cover.'

'Then if you've got any better plan, spit it out.'

Kirk shrugged. He turned his eyes from the scene in front of him with reluctance, ran the tip of his tongue over his dry lips. 'All right. We'll hit 'em from two directions.' He motioned towards a boulder some twenty feet away to his right. 'Give me time to get there, then we'll finish the job.'

Laredo nodded to indicate that he had understood. Flattening himself to the ground, Kirk wriggled forward through the tall, stiff-standing grass, taking care to make no noise. For several yards he did not raise up, but moved with his head and shoulders well down, ears straining for the slightest sound from the direction of the clearing.

Not until he reached the cover of the boulder, did he lift himself a little, glanced back to where Laredo's indistinct figure lay prone behind the other rock. Then he eased his guns from their holsters, steadied himself against the smooth rock and peered cautiously over the top.

There were two men close to the horses on the far side of the clearing. The sentry, he noticed, was seated on the rock now, and the red tip of a cigarette glowed faintly against the shadowed blur of his face.

Smiling grimly to himself in the darkness, Kirk lifted the guns and laid the sights on the bunch of men in the middle of the clearing. Best to take them first and then concentrate on the others. Every single bullet had to count if they were to reduce the numbers of these men sufficiently to pin them down until the rest of the boys at the camp heard the racket and came running to see what was the cause of the shooting.

For a moment, a deep and pendant silence seemed to settle in a smothering blanket over everything. Then a horse threw up its head as if in sudden alarm and uttered a shrill neighing sound that broke the stillness, shattering it into a thousand screaming fragments. In the same instant, Kirk squeezed the triggers of the guns. The crash of the twin shots, sounding as a single sound, came in sharp, angry counter to the harsh yell of one of the men as he pitched forward on to his face in the long grass. A horse reared among the trees, thrashed with its flailing forepaws at the air, brought the steel-tipped hoofs crashing down on the unprotected head of one of the men standing nearby as he tried to move away.

Laredo began firing from the other direction, his guns roaring in the night. A man, staggering to his feet, clutched drunkenly at his stomach, stood swaying for a few moments, then went down without a sound. Another two crumpled into still things on the ground. The rest of the men scattered, ran for cover, some blindly, others dropping on to their faces and wriggling forward, presenting more difficult targets. Bullets began to come back at them from the clearing, striking the rocks which afforded them cover. A ricochet screeched wildly into the night with a thin, banshee wail that tore at Kirk's ears as he flinched instinctively.

Had the other men heard the din? Had they realised what was happening or did they intend to stick by the herd just in case it was a trap to trick them away from the cattle as had happened in the past?

The moon drifted behind a bank of clouds. In the ensuing darkness, a small group of the rustlers moved into deeper cover at the far side of the clearing. Kirk sent a couple of shots whistling after them, heard one of the men cry out. Almost immediately there was the sound of a heavy body falling into the brush, or it being dragged deeper into the undergrowth.

A hard, familiar voice yelled from the shadows: 'Don't let them get away. There are only two of them, behind those boulders. Keep them pinned down while the rest of us work around them. They can't get away.'

Kirk did not doubt that it had been Fleck who had yelled that harsh order. He glanced across at Laredo. Their position could be precarious if the rustlers did as the other ordered. They would only have to send a fusillade of bullets into the rocks to keep them trapped there while the others moved around on either flank.

Swiftly, he thumbed fresh shells into the guns. More slugs struck the top of the boulder and whined into the darkness in murderous ricochet. Leaving the dead fall in a crouched-over sprint, he went ducking and weaving from cover to cover as he ran back to where Laredo crouched behind the rock. To his right there were the slashing, stabbing bursts of gunfire among the trees and the evaluating appraisal he had made from his original position proved to be correct. The rustlers were clustered together in the undergrowth on the edge of the dim moonlight. The moon sailed fully into an open, clear patch of sky as he drew level with Laredo, dropped down beside the other.

'Quickly!' he snapped. 'Get back to the horses. Once they move around us, we're finished.' As he spoke, he sent a couple of shots after a dark figure that flitted from one tree to another, saw the man jerk as lead nicked his arm, then run on.

Laredo muttered something under his breath, moved with an obvious reluctance. Bending, Kirk caught him tightly by the arm, hauled him to his feet. There were still too many of the rustlers in the clearing for them to be able to take care of them. The element of surprise had worn off, the outlaws had been warned of their presence and it had not taken Fleck long to realise just how many men there were facing them. The foreman would also know that the men down at the camp would have heard the din and might, even at that moment, be riding hell for leather to see what it was all about. He had to make his move quickly and destroy Laredo and himself before the others had a chance to get there and throw the weight of their gunfire into the battle.

Gunfire from the trees was almost deafening as they gathered their legs under them, whipped upright off the stony ground, and began to run powerfully back along the winding track. Shots followed them all the way, screeching along the flinty walls of the trail with the scream of tortured metal. Whirling to cover the other, Kirk loosened off a couple of shots as wild yells lifted from the faint moonlight behind them. The sounds of gunfire were unremitting and thunderous.

At a bend in the track he paused long enough to draw down a great gulp of air and thumb back the hammers of the Colts, glancing swiftly behind him as Laredo stumbled forward over the uneven ground. Three men came into sight around the distant bend in the trail, passed over a stretch of moonlight, then paused as they sensed his presence there. Muzzle flashes bloomed redly in the dimness. There was a ripping, tearing sound as lead crashed though the rotting trunk of a solitary tree that jutted out from the bank of earth nearby. Kirk fired, spun away from the spot and thumbed off another shot as Laredo yelled at him to pull back.

One of the rustlers gave up a loud cry, any words indistinguishable in the thundering tumult, but his tone was that of a man badly hurt and shaken. Ducking back swiftly, he found Laredo crouched within a narrow cleft in the solid rock. It was as good a defensive position as any and he dropped down beside the other, thrusting cartridges into the chambers of the guns as the other wriggled into a position where he could see clearly along the trail at this point.

'They seem to be debatin' whether to come any further or not,' grunted the oldster. His eyes glittered in the faint moonlight that shafted down into the trail cut through this neck of the rocky ledge. 'You must've scared 'em real bad.'

'I dropped one of 'em as they came along the trail,' Kirk said, breathing heavily. He cast a quick glance about him. 'But if they do, we may not be able to hold 'em off for long.'

'Maybe we won't have to,' said the other. He lifted his head a little, cocked it on one side, listening intently.

Kirk tried to pick out whatever it was the other had heard. For a moment, there was nothing but the faint soughing of the wind as it rustled through the bending grass. Then he heard, far off, but coming swiftly nearer, the thudding of hoofs, somewhere down in the valley.

The rustlers must have heard that sound too and realised what it portended, for a man shouted harshly: 'Those cowboys are headin' this way, Telfer. We've lost too many men to hold 'em off if they get up here.'

A pause, then Telfer's voice yelling: 'Finish off those two and then let's ride back into the hills.'

'Ain't no time to finish 'em.' There was anxiety and apprehension in the man's voice. 'Those *hombres* are nearly here.'

More gunfire broke out from the men holed up at the bend in the trail. Bullet after bullet skipped and tore against the rocky wall on either side of the cleft. Splinters of stone struck Kirk's face and he felt the warm stickiness of blood on his cheek. Breathing hard, he flattened himself against the rock, edged his head forward a little until he could just make out the stabbing muzzle blasts from the guns. There were only two men back there, he judged, although in the moonlight it was difficult to be sure. He stood there for a moment considering what course of action to pursue. If either of those two men worked his way a little further around to the other side of the trail, he would be able to fire directly into the cleft and they would be unable to move. Gunpowder clouded the air, making it hard to see clearly, but he caught a vague glimpse of one man moving back, firing from the hip as he did so. Snapping a couple of quick shots at him, he tried to make out where the other man was hidden. Then the brisk rattle of gunfire from just beyond the edge of the trail sounded, blotting out all other noise. The rustlers pulled back rapidly towards the clearing a hundred yards away. Kirk stepped boldly out into the open trail as the first of the riders broke into view some fifty yards away.

Blaine's voice yelled harshly: 'Hold your fire, men. It's Brennan.'

They reined up and Laredo, moving beside Kirk, pointed along the trail. 'Get after 'em,' he ordered. 'Follow 'em, damn you, and ride 'em down.'

Whistling up his own mount, Kirk swung into the saddle, rode back along the trail and through the wide, stony clearing. There were three or four bodies visible among the rocks, but no sigh of the rest of the rustlers. One by one, the others came riding back.

'They've pulled back into the hills,' said Blaine tightly. 'We'd never have a chance of finding 'em there. Too many Indian trails they could have taken and nobody here can follow sign in moonlight. They must have a camp some-where back there.' He jerked a thumb in the direction of the high peaks that lifted above the wooded slopes.

Kirk nodded, thrust the Colts back into their holsters, looked round at Laredo and then down at the dead men stretched on the rocks and rough grass. 'I'd say this was a good night's work,' he said slowly. 'Guess Cantry might recognise some of these men if they were taken back into town for identification. That is, if he's a mind to. Could be that if Culver doesn't want any of 'em recognised, Cantry will never have seen any of 'em before.'

One of the men laughed harshly, cynically. 'You're right there mister,' he acknowledged. 'But I figure we should take 'em in. Somebody might talk.'

Laredo slipped from the saddle, peered into the face of each dead man in turn, then shook his head as he mounted up again. 'Ain't seen any of 'em myself,' he admitted. 'They could all be strangers here. Culver ain't likely to pick men who're known well in this territory.'

'I heard one of them called by his name,' Kirk said slowly. 'Telfer.'

Laredo pondered the name for a moment, then shrugged, pursing his lips. 'It means nothin' to me,' he said finally. The rest of the men shook their heads in unison.

# CHAPTER FIVE

# GUNSLINGER

While two of the men took the bodies of the slain rustlers back into Wasatch, Kirk remained with the herd. There seemed little possibility that the rustlers would make any further attempt on the cattle now that the sting had been taken from them during the gun battle in the hills. Kirk had the feeling that Culver would find it difficult to get more men to ride with the outlaw band he had formed in the hills if one word of this leaked out. As for the dead men who had been taken back into town, he would have to ensure that no one who might recognise any of the men, talked about it.

On the fourth night, rolled in his blanket close to the fire, he lay with his hands clasped behind his head, staring up at the pitch blackness of the sky, with the bright stars sprinkled like diamonds on a velvet backcloth, thinking things out in his mind. Normally, after a hard day's work in the saddle, he found no difficulty in going to sleep, but tonight seemed different. He realised that although he had helped in no small way to smash one of Culver's bands and give a jolting setback to his plans, he was still no closer to getting his own revenge on the other for what had happened ten years before.

The immediate desire to meet the other face to face and destroy him in one swift, savage stroke, had faded somewhat from his mind and he had grown to accept the fact that when he did meet up with the other, Culver would have to face the fact of his own guilt, recognize who it was who faced him, finding his own ruin within himself in that moment before he went into eternity.

A few feet away, Laredo rolled over in his blankets and in the red fire glow, Kirk was able to see the other's face turned towards him. 'What's the matter, Kirk? Can't you sleep either?'

'Too much on my mind, maybe.' Kirk made an irritated grunt. 'I keep thinkin' about Culver, wonderin' when I'm goin' to get a chance at him. So long as I'm lyin' out here that ain't likely. And those men we sent back into Wasatch. Even though they were dead, they might have told us a lot.'

Laredo shook his head. 'Culver's far too clever for that. Every gunslinger on his payroll will have been brought in from Texas or even somewhere south of the border in New Mexico. He's got to consolidate his position in Wasatch before he can afford to get careless. He hasn't got where he is today, by takin' chances.'

'Could be you're right,' Kirk acknowledged grudgingly. 'All I know is that the sooner I can get back into town and snoop around there for a while, the easier I'll feel in my mind. I've still got a score to settle with the townsfolk. They were mostly damned eager to join Culver in stringin' me up when they had that lynchin' party out in the streets.'

'Memories are pretty short with most folk,' Laredo said quietly. 'You'll find that many of them will have forgotten your name. Even Cantry who may have a picture of you filed away in one of his drawers, will have forgotten you until he checked with his wanted notices.'

'That doesn't excuse them for what they did,' Kirk said

grimly. 'They wanted to hang me without a trial, without even a chance to speak in my own defence. Are you sayin' that I should forget that, overlook it as if it had never happened?'

'No; but I do say that you ought to take things a mite easy when you do get back in town. Don't go shootin' off your mouth or pickin' quarrels with everybody who may have been in that lynchin' party ten years ago. Chances are they won't know what you're talkin' about unless you deliberately remind 'em.'

There was a faint challenge in the other's words; a challenge that waited for an answer from the man who lay silent in his blankets. Kirk lay silent for several moments, turning ideas over in his mind. It was almost as though he had not heard the other's words. At length, Laredo turned to look at him closely.

'Don't you agree that would be the best course, Kirk?'

'That they may not remember me – yes,' Kirk said at length.

'And the rest of it?'

'I'm not interested in whether they recall who I am or not,' Kirk said slowly. 'I've got somethin' to do and I mean to do it, all the way. When you've lived with hate and the thought of revenge for as long as I have, hunted and outlawed for something you've never done, then you can imagine how I feel about these people and Culver in particular.'

Laredo grinned thinly. 'All of which sounds as though you've thought of nothin' else. Ten years is a long time to live with only hate. It can warp and twist a man like nothin' else.'

'You sound as though you've experienced it yourself,' Kirk murmured. He lay for a while listening to the distant sounds of the herd as they moved a trifle restlessly in their bedding ground.

'I know what it can do,' said the other evenly. 'I had a

brother once. He got into a crooked card game with some river gamblers, called out a man who was cheating him. He didn't really know how to use a gun, never had a chance. But somebody shot him in the back before he could pull his sixgun from its holster. That was the sort of hatred I had to live with until I rode down the killer, smoked him out into the open.'

'You killed him?'

Laredo gave a brusque nod. 'I killed him in fair fight, but it didn't make the difference I thought it would. I'd avenged my brother's murder, but there was no peace in my mind. There was just a feeling of emptiness that was almost as bad as the hate I'd been forced to live with.'

'I'll remember that when I face Matt Culver,' Kirk said shortly. He felt a sudden coldness on his face and a tightening of the muscles of his chest. A moment later, he turned over on to his back. There was a vague yellow glow in the east where the moon, a little past full, was beginning to rise. It was, he judged, already after midnight.

After a pause, Laredo said softly: 'We'll be ridin' back into town day after tomorrow. Could be you'll get your chance then. But be careful. There are eyes and ears everyplace in Wasatch, and every one of them reports back to Culver or Cantry, and in town that means the same thing.'

'I'll watch my step.' He recognised the wisdom of what the other had said.

Two days later, three of them began the long ride back to Manson's ranch and then on into Wasatch with their wages. With Kirk went Laredo and Blaine. On the ride, Kirk felt Laredo watching him covertly as they rode, but it was impossible to guess at the thoughts which were running through the other's mind. Here, in the cattle country, there was one common denominator among the men who rode for the various ranches – loyalty. So long as they took the pay of any particular man, they remained loyal to that man, they did everything that was required of them whether or not it was in or out of the law. Usually, when the law was as corrupt as it appeared to be in Wasatch it made little difference and even men like Kirk had no difficulty in reconciling their actions with their consciences.

It was just possible that Laredo was a little uncertain about him, knowing how badly he wanted to destroy Culver and everything that belonged to the other. It might be that this desire for vengeance did not tally with the loyalty which Manson required of his men. Laredo was a cattleman, foremost and simple. It was doubtful if he could really see beyond that fact. He could not understand how a man could want to use his position, working for a man like Manson, to get at Culver.

The afternoon was half gone and the heat head had reached its zenith of piled-up intensity, lay like a smothering blanket over the plain as they came within sight of the low hills which almost encircled the Manson place. Kirk let his breath go in slow pinches through his nostrils as he sighted the undulating hills on the skyline, repressed the urge to send his mount racing forward and fought down the restlessness in his mind. Men such as Culver were playing for keeps and there was no way, as yet, of knowing what had been happening in Wasatch during the few days he had been away. It was possible that those riders who had checked in at the hotel a few moments after he had pulled out that first morning, had indeed been looking for him, trying to check on him, asking for the register to make a note of the name written there. Fleck might also have delivered a report on him to Matt Culver.

With an effort, he pushed the thoughts out of his mind, concentrated on the present. Rubbing the sweat and dust from his eyes, he felt each breath go down like fire into his heaving lungs. Here, nothing relieved the terrible, burning pressure of the heat, the harsh smell of burnt sage that drifted up from the ground about them and mingled with the acrid dust. Riding was a long, seemingly endless, punishment. Every breath was a labour, a sucking in of superheated air that hurt the chest and provided little refreshment to the body.

An hour later, they rode down the gentle slope of one of the hills, into the hard, sun-baked earth of the court-yard in front of the Manson ranch. Dropping wearily from the saddle, Kirk eased stiff legs and walked with the other two men towards the porch where Manson was waiting for them.

The other stepped down to meet them. 'You did a good job back there,' he said, his gaze flicking from one man to the other. 'The boys came through a few days ago with those men you killed. We may have smashed Culver's rustlin' band for good. Could be they won't bother us again.'

'I wouldn't bank on it,' Kirk said roughly. 'That was only a small gang we surprised. The next time, they won't be so easy to take. Somehow, I don't think this is goin' to make Culver stop his attacks on you. He may have to change his plans a little but that's all.'

Manson gave him a quick look. Then he nodded, his lips tight. 'Well, I guess you've all earned your pay this time. You'll be wantin' to ride on into Wasatch.'

Laredo nodded. 'I figure we can make it before dark,' he said.

Manson hesitated, then threw a glance at Kirk. 'Culver will know by now that you had a hand in this,' he said sombrely. 'He may not make trouble with any of my other riders, but he'll sure make a try for you. Be careful. A slug can come from anywhere in town. And they'll just as surely shoot you in the back as call you.'

'I'm expectin' it,' Kirk said. He went towards the bunkhouse with the rest of the men, washed under the pump in the courtyard, knocked the grey-white dust from his shirt and pulled it on again. He waited for the others, then swung into the saddle.

An hour later, with the sun lowering towards the peaks that lifted from the plains far to the north-west, they came within sight of the squat buildings of Wasatch, with the dusty white streak of the north-south road running straight through the town from one end to the other, vanishing beyond the furthermost outskirts into the hills. Touching spurs to their mounts, they rode faster, with the thoughts of the saloons and gambling houses spurring them on. For men who rode the herds many miles from these outposts of civilisation, every moment they had to spend in town was doubly precious.

Once in Wasatch, they scattered. Kirk reined his mount halfway along the main street, cast a quick look about him, then slid from the saddle, moved on to the boardwalk. The tenseness was back in his mind, tightening the muscles of his body. His gaze flicked towards every move-ment in the growing dusk and he felt more jumpy and edgy than usual.

One thing was quite clear. He meant to discover if there was any proof that Culver was tied in with that rustling party he and Laredo had scattered up there in the hills a couple of nights earlier. There was sure to be talk of some kind in town about it, even now and if he kept his eyes and ears open he might be able to learn a lot. Once he had the sort of information he wanted, then he would try to find where Cantry stood with respect to Matt Culver. If, as he was now beginning to suspect, the two were in cahoots with each other, then he would have to make his plans accordingly. But first, he needed proof of Culver's guilt.

He let enough time elapse to feel safe, keeping to the narrow side alleys until it became really dark. There were plenty of riders drifting into town once the sun had gone down and he recognised the Double Lance brand on several of the mounts tied up outside the saloon. He made

99

a slow-swinging search of the town, estimating how many Double Lance riders were there and roughly where they were.

He stepped clear of the lighted windows of a couple of stores, noticed the men inside, checking over their account books, arranging some of their wares for the next day, then moved across the dimly-lit street to the saloon on the far side. A small group of men were standing on the boardwalk several yards away, talking loudly and vehemently among themselves. All appeared to be Double Lance men but at the moment, none of them seemed interested in anything but their argument. Kirk had no difficulty in imagining what the outcome would be if he was recognised. It was extremely likely that he had been seen by the man named Telfer during that attack in the hills. He did not think the gunman would forget his face if that was indeed the case.

Pushing open the swing doors of the saloon with the flat of his hand, he went inside, blinking for a moment at the bright light. More than a score of lanterns hung from the low ceiling and there were others behind the long bar which ran almost the full length of one side of the room. Already, poker and faro games were in progress at several of the tables and there were men standing against the counter. Except for exchanging a few looks with some of the men, Kirk did not speak as he went over to the bar and rested his elbows on it, lifting one finger to the nearer of the two barkeeps. The man came over, picked a bottle from under the counter and set it in front of him, together with a glass. Kirk poured himself a drink, then clapped his fingers around the bottle as the other made to take it away.

'Just leave it there,' he said quietly. 'I've ridden a long way in the last few days and I've got a lot of drinking to make up.'

The other stared at him closely for a long moment, the look on his face both angry and truculent. Evidently he did not recognise the man who stood in front of him, but there was something about the other which made him back down. He moved away along the counter, flicking at it with his wet cloth. Something told the barkeep that this man might be slouching there over the bar right now, but he could be trouble four ways from Sunday if the need ever arose. Kirk drank his drink slowly, listening to the laughter and shouts from the other tables, at the talk that went on a little further along the bar. He did not recognise any of the men in the saloon by sight although it was possible that any might have been in that bunch who had tried to rustle the cattle way up on the north range.

He had been there for perhaps fifteen minutes when the door opened and two men swaggered in. Both were Double Lance riders judging from the way they were greeted by others at the various tables and along the bar. Kirk eyed them both narrowly, saw them bend their glance on him as they came forward. Then they appeared to take no further notice of him, leaning against the bar, talking in low voices.

Tilting the bottle, he poured himself another drink, raised it to his lips, then stiffened a little as he glimpsed through the crystal mirror at the back of the bar, the man who entered though the doors. There was no mistaking Fleck, the Double Lance foreman.

The other came forward, his gaze sliding from man to man. It lingered for a long moment on Kirk, then a faint gust of expression went over his features and he moved close to the other, placing himself between Kirk and the other two men along the counter.

'You still in town, mister?' he said thinly. There was a note of menace in his voice. 'Seems to me I recall givin' you a warnin' some days ago when we last met.'

'You know, you seem downright inhospitable,' Kirk said quietly, tossing down his drink. He turned slightly to face the other. 'Just what you got on your mind, Fleck?'

'You got a pretty short memory,' said the other, after a momentary pause. 'I offered you a good job ridin' for the Double Lance outfit. You turned it down even when I told you not to be in town after sundown if you did that. Now it just occurs to me you might not have heard me right the last time.'

Kirk lowered his gaze a little, noticed where the other's left arm had been bandaged and something clicked into place in his mind. He said thinly: 'I see you've been injured, Fleck. Could it have been a scratch from a bullet while you were up in the hills overlookin' the north range – Manson's spread?'

Fleck's eyes narrowed to flinty slits and his lips were parted a little, showing his teeth. He sucked in a sharp breath, then said tautly: 'Just what have you got on your mind, friend? You seem to be determined to push yourself where you're not wanted. Here in Wasatch, we don't like people who do that and we have our own ways of dealin' with 'em.'

'So I can guess.' There was a faintly sneering touch to Kirk's tone. Even though he did not remove his gaze from the other, he knew that most of the play at the tables had ceased and that the other customers were intent on watching what was happening at the bar. 'I know for myself the sort of judgement that the people of Wasatch can hand out. By now, though, most everybody will have seen those dead men who were brought into town by the Manson boys a couple of days ago, and they'll know that we smashed one of your attempts to raid the Manson herd. That wound in your arm looks suspiciously like one I gave one of the rustlers myself.'

'You tryin' to insinuate that I was ridin' with those rustlers?' snarled the other harshly. His right hand hovered close to the butt of the gun in his belt. 'There are plenty of men here who'll be witnesses as to where I was when that raid was supposed to have taken place.'

'I've no doubt about that, Fleck,' said Kirk evenly. 'And they'll all be liars like yourself, gunslingers brought into the territory by Culver to make sure he can take over every other ranch whenever he sets his mind to it. Only I know that one of the men in that gang was called Telfer, heard him called by name several times as did the other men with me, and when I find him, I've got ways of making him talk.' He grinned viciously. 'And he's goin' to tell me that you were there and that Culver paid you to raid the herds of the other ranchers like he did seven years ago when he took most of Old Man Herdson's cattle and then forced him to sell out.'

'I've never heard of the name,' said Fleck harshly. He spoke to the rest of the men in the room without turning his head or taking his eyes off Kirk. 'Anybody here heard of a hombre named Telfer?'

His question was answered by shakes of the head from all of the others. Kirk kept his gaze levelly on the foreman. The negative attitude was so false that he took no notice of it, merely said: 'You're not convincin' anybody with that kind of talk.'

The other's coarse features were briefly impassive, then they began to darken into a scowl. 'No?' Turning, he stared round at the rest of the men, then looked back. 'I know who you are, mister. Your name's Kirk Brennan, the *hombre* who killed some fella on the trail and then bust out of jail after bein' arrested for murder and rustlin'. I seem to remember that was quite a few years ago, but I reckon the warrant is still in force. Ain't nothin' lower than a critter who shoots another man in the back.'

Kirk waited, knowing that the other was hungering for a fight, looking for trouble; seeing it in the foreman's bearing, in his attitude, the identical stance and look he had seen on many occasions in the past. Fleck was battle-scarred and competent looking and had evidently survived plenty of violence, otherwise he would never have got to be foreman under Culver.

'You'd better back off, Fleck,' Kirk said tightly. 'I don't want to have to kill you before I have to. My fight is with Culver, not with you. And I notice you've got a score of guns at the back of you, though maybe those are the sort of odds you like.' He deliberately made his tone insolent and insulting, saw the red flush spread up from the other's bull-like neck, knew that he had touched a sore spot.

Fleck growled a loud oath, moved away from the bar, but he made no move to go for his guns. Instead, he said thinly: 'Never mind about the others, Brennan. This is between you and me. Shuck that gunbelt and I'll grind your face in the dirt.' He moved flat-footedly forward, unbuckling his own gunbelt as he moved.

Kirk watched him narrowly for a long moment, then allowed his glance to flicker swiftly over the other's shoulder at the rest of the Double Lance riders in the saloon, wondering whether they would join in if it were seen that he was getting the upper hand. He saw few men who were evidently not riding for Culver there, knew that he would be hopelessly outnumbered if he should beat the other in a fist fight, that he would never have a chance to pick up his gunbelt before the riders could cover him and drop him without trouble.

Then there was a sudden movement at the far end of the counter. The bartender there had thrust his hand unnoticed under the bar and come up with a dangerous-looking shotgun which he held capably in his hands, levelling it at the men near the tables.

'They won't give you any trouble, mister,' he said ominously. 'Not if they want to stay alive.'

Kirk saw the quick look of anger pass over Fleck's face. The other said in a stony voice. 'I'll remember this, Hank. That was a very foolish thing to do.'

'Maybe so,' said the other evenly. 'But I like to see a

man get a fair shake of the dice. This will even up the odds a little and as I remember it, you called him out to a fist fight.'

There was no alternative for Kirk. Fleck was committed now; and he unbuckled his gunbelt slowly, letting it slide towards the floor, then kicking it away from the middle of the floor over against the bar. Fleck came forward, arms swinging a little, his broad body in a half-crouch, muttering oaths all of the time. It was an old trick and Kirk was not fooled by it. The other was trying to hold his attention while he made to swing a hard fist at his head. Rocking forward slightly on the balls of his feet, he was ready as the other swung a roundabout blow at him all the way from his knees. It missed as Kirk had intended that it should and as the foreman swayed to one side, temporarily off balance by the force of his swing, Kirk was ready. Twisting slightly, he unleashed a couple of powerful body blows that sank deep into the other's midriff, sending the air whistling in a thin bleat of agony through his parted lips. Fleck's eyes glazed a little as he staggered under the impact of the blows and his cheeks were drawn right down on to the bones of his face as he tried to pull air down into his tortured lungs. The foreman was rocked. Lowering his head to hide it from any other blow that might be on its way, he crowded forward, seeking to pin Kirk back against the bar with his body. There was sweat beading his forehead, trickling into his eyes and he shook his head angrily to dash it away. Kirk did not remove his gaze from the bigger man, was ready as the other moved, with a surprising agility in a man of his bulk, swinging round boring in low with a series of jabbing punches. It was inevitable as he moved in close, that some of them should get through and Kirk felt them hammer solidly against his chest, threatening to crush his ribs to pulp. He sucked in air, forced his blurring vision to fight itself, and moved round as the other's knee came up sharply, so that it struck his thigh and not his groin as it was intended.

Fleck planted both his feet firmly together, bracing himself against the bar, his hair falling over his eyes, lips open, showing his teeth in an animal-like snarl. He shook off the pain that must have been in his body, swung his arms again, sensing victory in his grasp. When Kirk did not retreat, he threw a flurry of blows, boring in savagely, only to be brought up with a jolt as Kirk got through his guard and planted several short jabs in the other's face. He felt the man's nose go under his fist, saw the blood spurt from it. Fleck muttered something indistinguishable under his breath and gave ground slowly.

Then Kirk made his first mistake. Driving in two more solid blows, he waited a few seconds too long before moving back, out of range of the other. Fleck seemed to have anticipated his move on this occasion and with a sudden swiftness, lunged forward, head butting at Kirk's chest, arms flung wide, encircling him around the small of his back, bearing him backwards against one of the low tables.

A chair gave under their combined weight, the wood splintering and there was a grin of bestial triumph on Fleck's face as he bore down on the other man, thrusting him back over the top of the heavy table, fingers linked behind Kirk's back as he began to squeeze with all of his strength, his head thrust into Kirk's chest to add every ounce of weight to his attempt to break his spine. Instinct made Kirk relax as the other thrust forward, his face averted to protect his eyes if the other should suddenly make a try for them. He knew that he had to break this hold or it would be the end of him. Vaguely, above the roaring of blood pounding through his forehead and the ringing in his ears, he heard the men in the saloon yelling encouragement to Fleck. He hoped that the man at the back of the counter still kept that shotgun trained on them.

106

For a moment, he did not move, allowing his body to go limp. This had the desired effect of forcing Fleck off balance again, making it impossible for him to draw his arms as tightly as he wished. Before the other could adjust his grip, Kirk had thrown his body sideways, off the side of the table. He struck the floor hard, with a shuddering impact that knocked all of the wind from his lungs, but he was twisted sideways now, and Fleck's weight was no longer on him. Reaching up with his hands, he thrust the heel of his right hand under the foreman's chin, exerting all of his strength as he forced the man's head back. Fleck struggled to keep his advantage, striving to tighten his encircling grip, but slowly, inexorably, his head was thrust back as Kirk heaved upwards. Gradually, the other's arms began to loosen their hold. He was able to draw air down into his lungs again and the throbbing in his head eased slowly.

The foreman gasped and writhed. Each second, the pressure on his face increased and the pain and suffocation became more intense, more difficult to bear until finally, he was forced to slacken his grip around Kirk's wrist as he tried to force his arm away. His eyes were bulging from their sockets, his mouth pressed tightly together so that the other's nostrils were flared as he tried to breathe.

Drawing back his left arm, Kirk slammed a hard blow into the other's exposed adam's apple. The man uttered a faint gurgle of agony and went limp, his throat muscles virtually paralysed by the single blow. His eyes glazed and he did not get to his feet as Kirk stood up, looking down at him, ready to make any further move if Fleck did get up. But the other continued to lie there, his head lolling stupidly to one side as he tried to rub his throat with his fingers, massaging it gently, all of the fight knocked out of him. Slowly, Kirk lifted his head and stared round at the circle of men in the saloon. Not one of them made any move towards his gun and out of the corner of his eye, he saw with a faint sense of relief that the barrel of the shotgun was still held on them.

Bending, he picked up his own gunbelt from where it had come to rest near the bar, buckled it on, eased the sixguns slowly in their holsters, then stepped over Fleck's inert form.

'When he comes round fully,' he said to the others, 'I reckon you'd better warn him that it won't be long before I've got all the proof I need and when I have, he'd better be ready, because I'll come gunnin' for him, and any of you who are still around. Culver's reign in this territory is rapidly comin' to an end. Better get out while you still have the chance.'

He moved slowly towards the door, paused as he reached it. He was suddenly acutely aware that the two Double Lance riders who had been standing near the bar were no longer there, that during the fighting, they had slipped out. He did not have to think twice as to why they had done this, nor where they had gone. They had ridden along the main street to locate Culver who was probably in town someplace.

He knew that he had to keep moving; that very soon, the rest of the Double Lance riders would start hunting him down in town and there were very few places where it would be safe for him to hide. Very likely, Culver would have blocked the road out of town, making it impossible for him to get out. The ways of violence were never changing even though this was no longer a frontier town and there was a semblance of civilisation on the surface of everyday life. But it was only a thin veneer and beneath it, death and terror were beginning to uncoil themselves like a rattler in this small town.

Culver's men would soon be scattering through the street and narrow alleys of Wasatch. They would probably have found his mount, were perhaps watching every Manson horse in town. They would not openly seek trouble with the other Manson riders. The time for that was not quite at hand. Culver wanted to be really ready before he started a range war. But hunting down one man was a very different matter.

He crossed slowly over the street until he reached a wealth of gloom between two of the taller buildings. Here he paused briefly for breath and his bearing, striving to pick out landmarks which had changed little in ten years. He saw a bunch of men move out of the swing doors of the saloon, their figures outlined briefly against the flood of light from the bar. Hesitating for a moment, they then spread out, moving along both directions of the street. Several held drawn guns in their hands. He moved back around the edge of the boardwalk. There was no chance at all of reaching his horse. Not a big chance of getting clear either. Turning, he darted down the blackness of the alley, hearing the shouts of the men at his back as they began to search for him, probably with the incentive of a bonus for the man who brought him in, dead or alive.

He was almost at the end of the alley when he heard the warning shout behind him. Turning, he had a glimpse of a compact mass of men moving into the opening which led off the main street, swinging in behind him. A ragged volley of gun blasts, sounding unnaturally loud in the confined space of the alley rang in his ears and he sprinted madly for the far end of the opening, ducking behind the wall of the old warehouse that loomed up on his left. Bullets hammered off the walls near him. There was the feel of a red-hot brand laid on his upper arm as a slug scorched along his flesh. He jerked instinctively, lifted his guns and fired six quick shots into the dimness, then thumbed fresh shells into the empty chambers. The metal of the guns was hot under his fingers.

A man stumbled and fell with a harsh shout and the rest of the Double Lance gunhawks drew back, giving Kirk a brief, but precious, respite. In the pitch blackness here among empty, deserted buildings, low-roofed and window-less, he moved away from the end of the alley, working his way along the walls of the storehouses. The shadows were dense on either side of the taller buildings here and he kept into them. Fifteen yards along, he came on to a low fence that stretched from one building to another. He had no other choice but to haul himself over it and the moment he did so, he knew that it had been a wrong move on his part for it outlined him on the skyline, only for a second or so, but long enough for a sharp-eyed man halfway along the alley to spot him and sing out a warning to the others.

'There he is! Goin' over the fence yonder.' The man's yell was punctured by a sudden shot and a bullet sang close to Kirk's head as he dropped over the other side of the fence, landed hard, picked himself up and began to run, hearing the pounding of feet close behind him on the hard ground. The fence was of the open kind and provided him with no cover as the men began firing, guns blazing in the night. Kirk gritted his teeth as he scrambled savagely to one side, went down on one knee and commenced to return the fire. The cluster of men scattered as the slugs tore in among them; all except for one man who came running blindly to the fence, firing as he ran.

'Keep your fool head down,' yelled one of the men to the rear. 'He's armed and we probably ain't hit him yet.'

'Like hell you haven't,' thought Kirk harshly, aiming at the looming shape of the man near the fence. He squeezed the trigger gently, felt the gun buck against his wrist, saw the man stagger, clutch wildly at his chest as he fell back, the guns slipping from his nerveless fingers, clattering to the ground as he went down. He was dead before he hit the ground.

'Danged fool,' said the man who had shouted the warning earlier. 'Our best chance now is to swing around and cut him off. He can't get out of that warren of alleys no matter how hard he tries. Send in a crossfire to keep him pinned down.'

Crouching down as low as possible, Kirk blended himself with his background, eyes narrowed as he strove to pick out the men beyond the fence. He knew that it was just a matter of time before they had swung around in a wide arc, cutting off any retreat he might have. He knew that the man who had called out would not have warned him that there was no way out unless he was supremely confident of the fact himself.

Glancing behind him, he noticed where a store had partly collapsed, one of the walls fallen in crumbling ruin into the alleyway which bordered the building. Wriggling forward, he made the cover of the fallen masonry without drawing a further shot, but barely had he thrown himself down behind it than a savage crossfire burst around him, the bullets smacking the earth around his body. His best chance was to get out of this area of town, move out to the perimeter where most of the buildings were unoccupied, but he would have to move fast, otherwise those men who were swinging around him, would flank him and prevent any move among the buildings.

A gun roared loudly, and then another, as he rose to his feet, edged back towards the looming bulk of one of the warehouses. There was a ripping, tearing sound as slugs hit the dry wood, splintered it. He got to within a foot of the door set in the long wall, kicked it open, then stepped inside. Here, the roar of the gunfire did not sound as loud as it had outside, but there was another sound which sent chills racing along his spine as he edged forward in the pitch blackness. Bullets zipped through the flimsy wooden walls around him.

Stumbling forward, with the smell of decay and rotten-ness in his nostrils, he felt in front of him with one outstretched hand, touched something hard and unyielding, explored it rapidly and found that it was a ladder lead-ing up to the upper floor. He waited no longer, knowing that the men would be moving in on him as soon as they realised he had slipped away from them and there was little danger of return fire hitting them.

Stepping up to the loft ladder, he made his way up it, picking his way carefully as the wooden supports creaked ominously under his weight. When his upward groping fingers found no further rungs to cling to, he pulled himself forwards with a quick heave of his arms, shot a rapid look about him. There was a patch of darkness which did not seem to be so intense as the rest that lay about him, and edging cautiously forward, he came to the oblong opening in the upper wall which looked down on to the rear of the buildings. While the gunfire was making a sieve of the lower half of the building, none of the bullets came up here as yet and he stepped boldly towards the opening, peering out into the night. It was, he reck-oned, a forty foot drop to the ground below and there seemed no way down. Swiftly, he glared along the wall on either side, then noticed the narrow wooden ledge which ran along the outside of the building. It was less than two feet in width and looked broken and unsafe, but it was his only chance. Already, there was the sound of voices imme-diately below him.

Someone yelled thickly: 'He must've gone in here.' The words echoed around the walls of the room below. 'Find the ladder and we'll take a look upstairs.'

'Here's Jake with a lantern,' called another man.

Glancing towards the trapdoor through which he had just scrambled, Kirk saw a palely flickering yellow glow, knew that it was only a matter of minutes at the most before they started warily up the ladder. He held on to the sides of the opening for a moment, then stepped out on to the wooden ledge, sucking in a deep breath as he entrusted the whole weight of his body to the planking. It creaked and swayed ominously under him and a chill passed through him congealing the sweat on his body. It needed only a small part of it to give way and he would be thrown into the alley below with more than sufficient force to break every bone in his body.

Inch by inch, he moved along it, not daring to lift his feet, but shuffling them forward. Sweat dripped into his eyes, made it difficult for him to see properly. Once, the plank bent, almost pitching him away from the wall and he clawed desperately for something to grip on to while he regained his balance. The seconds ticked by with an agonising slowness as he made his way to the very end of the wall. Not until he reached it did he see that his luck had held. There was a similar ledge around the wall of the adjoining building, but it meant a leap into the darkness of almost four feet. That drop of almost forty feet was still there, a yawning chasm which threatened to drag him down to his death. But it was the only chance he had, a risk he must take. Wind sighed between the two buildings, the coldness of it touching every part of his body, but his face and the palms of his hands where they were pressed against the hard roughness of the wall at his back, were moist and sticky and where the sweat had trickled down his face it had felt a salt taste on his lips. Drawing in a deep breath, he let it go. It was just possible that he had completely misjudged the distance in the darkness. If he had, then it would be the end of him.

There came the babble of voices from the loft he had just left. Evidently the men there had discovered that it was empty, although with the lantern they might spot his footprints in the dust. Once they came to that opening, saw the ledge, there was the chance they might realise how he had got out. He waited no longer. Getting his legs under him, he thrust strongly upward, launched himself out into the darkness of the night. For one wild moment, he thought he was not going to make it. He seemed to have fallen short of the other wall, to be dropping down into that terrible chasm between the two buildings. Then his hands struck hard against the wall, his feet hit the wooden ledge and he was pressing his chest so tightly against the rough boards that his ribs felt as if they had been smashed to a pulp inside his bruised chest. For several seconds, he could not move; but hung there, like a fly against a ceiling. Gradually, there came the realisation that he had made it. He whipped himself around slightly, moved crabwise along the wall until he came to an opening in the loft similar to that in the opposite building and crawled through it, the breath rasping painfully in his throat. Inside the loft, he sank back against the wall for a moment, drawing in a long breath, forcing his thumping heart into a slower, more normal, pace.

Going forward, he found the trapdoor, lowered himself down the ladder and went quickly towards the door, opening it gently, peering out into the darkness. He could see no one moving outside but there was the sound of plenty of activity from the neighbouring warehouse. He slid his body out through the door, pulling one of the Colts from its holster, holding it tightly in his right hand. Squirming through a narrow opening between two buildings, he moved away from where he judged the main street to be, working his way towards the outskirts of town. A blast of gunfire echoed from behind him and he swung round sharply. Through narrowed eyes, Kirk could just see the head and shoulders of two men running through one of the intersecting alleys in the distance. It was doubtful if they had seen him and he guessed they had been firing at shadows, itchy fingers on the triggers of their guns. Several men had been hit during the past few minutes and they were taking no unnecessary chances.

'What the hell's goin' on over there?' Fleck's bull-like voice roared from the direction of the warehouse.

'Thought we spotted him,' called one of the two men.

114

'Guess we were mistaken.'

'Then don't waste bullets,' called the other harshly. 'You're only givin' yourselves away. He must be around the front of these buildings somewhere. He can't get back to the main street for his mount. Spread out and move around.'

Kirk heard the footfalls of the two men as they moved cautiously forward. A moment later, he saw them as they edged across a stretch of open ground. Jerking up his Colt, his finger tightened on the trigger, took up the slack, then he relaxed without firing the shot. He could have killed both men, there was no doubt of that, but so far, they were not aware of his position and if he fired now he would give himself away.

Slowly, he made his way along a narrow, rotting plank between two low walls, found himself in an open square formed by the fronts of four buildings where the dark shadows lay square and layered one on top of the other from the standing stores and deserted houses with their low, slanting roofs. He stood stone-like for a moment in that empty, breathing dark, searching about him with eyes and ears as he tried to place every man on his trail. The drowning blackness was filled with tiny sounds, some real and others imagined and he held his breath until it hurt in his lungs, turning his chest on fire. Straining his vision for a glimpse of a shifting silhouette, he waited for several moments, then made out the faint movement at the edge of sight. There came the hard, solid sound of something metallic striking the wall a few yards away; then total silence closed down again, but Kirk had seen enough to realise that the man was working his way slowly and carefully in his direction. This must be one of the men ordered to circle around the area and move in from the rear.

Smiling grimly to himself, he pressed his back hard against the low wall, stood with the gun poised in his right fist. The man had not seen him, was edging forward with his head bent, peering intently into the dark that lay on the square. Another ten feet and he was level with Kirk. Some hidden sense seemed to warn him of his danger but by then it was too late. Kirk's arm lifted and then descended, the gun barrel striking the man behind the ear with a muffled, crunching thud. Catching him as he fell, Kirk lowered the unconscious man to the ground, stepped over the inert body, and ran soft-footed over the square and into the darkness beyond. Here the buildings were in even worse shape than the others he had seen. It was clear they had not been occupied for many years and the look and smell of decay hung everywhere. In spite of the tension that had been building up in his mind, Kirk was still able to assess his position objectively. Soon, Fleck and the others would find the man he had knocked cold, would know that he had managed to slip through the net they had cast for him. Then they would not rest until they had scoured the whole of Wasatch for him. He had to find a place where he was relatively safe until he could get out of town and back to the Manson ranch. He went forward, moving noiselessly among towering buildings that lifted tall and silent to the night sky, towards the bright stars which shone clearly in the velvet darkness.

By the time the moon lifted from the eastern horizon, he was moving on the very outskirts of the town, still not venturing beyond the houses and adobes, certain that the trails would be watched by more of Culver's men.

Crossing hurriedly into a backlot where the shadows thrown by the low moon were deep and black, he paused at a sudden sound. Whirling, the gun in his hand pointed, his finger hard on the trigger, he saw the faint movement. Then he stiffened and remained stone-like as the slender figure moved towards him. Where the silvery starshine lay on her face it was visible with a pale glow and her eyes regarded him widely.

'Kirk! I thought you might head this way after I heard

116

the shooting in town. Are you all right?'

'If you mean am I unhurt, the answer's yes,' he said softly. 'But this is no place for you, Emmy. Better go before they catch up with me and there's more shootin'.'

'If there is I can become part of it.' Her tone was suddenly hard and almost aggressive. It was then that he noticed she was carrying a heavy Winchester in her hands.

'Emmy,' he said sharply. 'I don't have time to explain, but we have to get away from here. Culver has put some of his men along the trails leadin' out of town and it won't be possible for me to get back to the Manson ranch where I've got myself a job.'

'You'd better come back with me,' she said at once, turning to lead the way. 'I know this town better than you do.'

Kirk caught at her arm, restraining her. 'Your home will be one of the first places they'll look for me,' he said tightly. 'It will have to be someplace else.

The girl pondered that for a moment, then nodded. 'I know,' she said, responding to the urgency in his tone. 'There is one place where these men won't look for you.'

'Where is it?' he asked.

'I'll take you there.' She moved away into the moon-thrown shadows. 'We'll talk when we get there.'

'You're gettin' yourself into somethin' that can be dangerous,' he murmured harshly, as he moved beside her.

'After what Matt Culver did to us, this is my fight,' she reminded him. She began to hurry as a man shouted somewhere in the near distance and the sound of gunshots reached their ears. 'Quickly! There's not time to argue. They'll be here soon.'

She led the way through a maze of alleys in which he would have been completely lost had he been forced to find his way alone, pausing as they came within sight of an old church, with a wooden cross standing tilted on one side on top of it. The girl pushed open the heavy, creaking door, still banded with straps of metal, stepped inside. Kirk followed close on her heels, into the dark and gloomy church front. Here the darkness seemed deeper than outside as he eased the door shut, blotting out all of the night sounds.

'They won't think of coming here,' whispered the girl softly. 'You're safe for the time being. But you'll have to get out of town as soon as possible.'

'Culver knows he can't afford to let me slip through his fingers again,' Kirk said harshly.

'Does he know who you are?'

'He does by now.'

'This town is crawling with his men. More and more of them have been moving in during the evening. I thought there might be something big afoot, but I never guessed they would be looking for you.'

Swiftly, Kirk explained what had happened when he and Laredo had surprised the bunch of rustlers before they had had a chance to attack the men guarding the herd. When he had finished, she nodded:

'I saw the Manson men ride in with the bodies of those dead men,' she said quietly. 'They were trying to find someone who could identify them. But I guess everyone is too afraid of Culver and nobody talked.'

Kirk rubbed his chin thoughtfully. 'That was what I was afraid of. I'm sure Fleck, Culver's foreman, was with that bunch in the hills. I nicked one of the rustlers in the arm and Fleck's wearin' a bandage right there at this moment. But that's no proof.'

'You won't find it easy to get proof of any kind against Culver,' said the girl seriously. Her face was sombre.

'Perhaps not,' Kirk began, 'But if I could—' He broke off sharply at a sudden sound beyond the thick door of the church. There was the noise of several men moving quickly, spurs dragging on the hard, gritty ground. The

118

murmur of voices reached them but it was impossible to distinguish any words.

'They're going on past,' whispered the girl softly. She gripped his arm as the movement of men outside the church began to fade slowly into the distance.

Kirk nodded, put his finger to his lips for silence and pressed his ear close to the thick oaken door. Gradually, all sound faded and he let his breath go through his lips.

'You're right,' he acknowledged tautly. He began to feel more at ease. It seemed the girl was right, that they would not look for him there. Then a sudden sound sent his heart thudding in his chest. The handle of the door began to turn very slowly and quietly. Quickly, he motioned the girl back, gripping the Colt tightly in his right hand, waiting.

The door opened a crack. There was a faint gust of wind that swirled briefly about them, then the man outside, getting bolder, opened the door still further, pushed his gunhand in front of him as he began to ease his body warily through the opening. He would not be able to see anything for a moment in the utter blackness inside the church and Kirk waited just long enough for the other's arm to extend into the interior of the church beyond the door before making his move. Grasping the man's wrist with his left hand, he jerked sharply, hauling the other off balance, bringing him pitching forward. Before the gunhawk could cry out, Kirk swung the gun as he had once before that night and the man went down on to his knees with only a faint blast of sound escaping through his lips. He lay quite still as Kirk closed the heavy door once more.

Bending, he turned the gunman over and peered closely into the upturned face.

'Do you know who it is?' asked Emmy quietly. She knelt beside him.

Kirk shook his head. 'Never seen this *hombre* before,' he

119

admitted. 'But when he comes to, we should be able to make him tell us his name.'

'What if some of his companions come back looking for him?'

'That's possible.' He continued quiet for a moment, then went on: 'It could be that I'll get some of the proof I want from this man if I can get him to talk.'

'You must be very careful,' warned the girl soberly. 'Culver has plenty of friends in town and Cantry may be one of them. He's still officially the law around here and you'll not find it easy to go against him. I know my father once tried to get word through to one of the US. Marshals, informing him of what had happened.'

'But the word didn't get through.'

Emmy shrugged, studying him closely. 'My feeling is that the telegraph man is also in Culver's pay. No word gets out of Wasatch without his say-so. That way, he can be sure there won't be any trouble he doesn't know about breaking on him without warning.'

'All very cleverly done,' Kirk said wryly. 'I'm just beginning to understand everythin' I'm up against. It makes things even more difficult than I'd figured. I came ridin' back to Wasatch with only one thing in mind – to meet up with Matt Culver and kill him for what he did to me ten years ago. If I could make the town realise how wrong it had been, how unjust, then I'd do that too. But I seem to have ridden into the middle of a range war and that's always a most dangerous position for any man.'

He made to say something more, but at that moment, the man on the cold, stone floor began to stir. Kirk reached down and caught him by the arm, twisting it painfully, half hauling the other to his feet, the arm pushed up behind his back.

Sobbing breath painfully into his lungs, the other tried ineffectually to wriggle away. He was still only barely conscious.

'Better talk before I break your arm,' Kirk said in a hissed tone. 'Who are you and who gave the order to come after me?'

'I don't know what you're talkin' about,' snarled the other thinly. He sucked in a gust of air as Kirk increased the pressure on his arm, forcing it sharply up the man's back, the flat of his hand almost directly between the shoulder blades. It was an extremely painful position, one which few men could bear for long; and the gunhawk was no exception. Brave when he moved with a gang of men, having the advantage of sheer numbers, he was a coward when it came to facing a man on less than even terms.

'It's up to you,' Kirk went on remorselessly. He thrust the other over a little, knelt his weight on the man's bent upthrust elbow. The other screamed thinly, tried to lash out at Kirk with his other hand, but it merely clawed at the air.

'I don't know anythin',' he cried thinly, through teeth tightly clenched in agony. 'Fleck gives the orders. I just carry 'em out. That's all.'

'Not quite,' Kirk went on. 'What's your name?'

There was a long silence, then the other muttered: 'Telfer – Clem Telfer.'

Very slowly, Kirk released his grip on the gunhawk's arm. He felt a sudden gush of emotion go through him as he sat back on his heels, glancing across at the girl. 'This is one of the men we want,' he said slowly. 'I reckon we can get all the proof we need from him once we've made him talk a little more about that band of rustlers we shot up a couple of nights ago.'

# CHAPTER SIX

## BRENNAN HITS OUT

'Get on your feet and move slow and easy,' Kirk said, prodding the other with the barrel of his gun. 'You can try to run if you've got a mind to, but I wouldn't advise it.' Reaching down, he slid the guns from the other's holsters, tossed them away into the darkness of the church. He saw the other shake his head. Telfer was not afraid but he was now unshakeably convinced of the sheer foolishness of such a move and Kirk knew he would obey every order he gave implicitly.

'You can't force me to try to run just so that you can shoot me in the back, Brennan,' he muttered harshly. 'Sooner or later, the rest of the boys will find you and it'll be the end of you and the girl. Herdson won't last long either when they learn he's been helpin' you – and then we'll take Manson and the others. Nobody can stop us now. We're too goddamned big.'

'I wouldn't bank on that,' Kirk told him tightly. He opened the door a little and peered watchfully out into the moonlight. The tiny square outside was deserted and there was no sound of men nearby. In the distance, on the other side of town, he could pick out vague yells and an occasional shot.

Telfer walked slowly through the silent houses, slump-shouldered, head low, staring down at the ground under his feet. Evidently his mind refused to work ahead and he was unsure of what was going to happen to him now.

When they came within sight of the house that stood a little way back from the road, he paused, then said with a faint beat of sardonic mirth in his hard voice: 'You ain't tryin' to keep me a prisoner here, are you, Brennan? I'd have figured you for more sense than that. When they don't find you back there, this is the next place they'll visit and once they've surrounded the house, you won't have a chance.'

'Just step inside and keep quiet,' said Kirk warningly. He jammed the muzzle of the Colt hard into the small of the outlaw's back, heard the sharp intake of breath as the man staggered towards the door. Emmy knocked softly on it and a moment later, it swung noiselessly open.

'It's all right, it's only us, Father,' whispered Emmy quietly. She stepped inside and Kirk pushed Telfer forward.

'Who's this?' asked Herdson, staring up at the outlaw in the pale lantern light.

'His name's Telfer,' Kirk told him. 'He's one of the men who was in that rustlin' gang in the hills. I've got men who can prove that.' Out of the corner of his eye, he saw the other's sardonic smile fade swiftly at that remark, knew the other as not feeling quite so sure of himself now. 'I reckon he can tell us quite a lot once we get him to talk.'

Telfer licked his dry lips, said with a show of bravado, 'I don't intend to tell you anythin', Brennan.'

'You'll talk,' Kirk promised him. He turned to Herdson. 'Do you think you could get him out of town and across to Manson's place? Culver will have men watchin' most of the trails out of town, lookin' for me.'

123

Herdson gave a quick nod. 'I'll get him there,' he said harshly. His tone was grim and cold. He placed his powerful and severe eyes on Kirk. 'But what about you? You can't stay here in Wasatch after what must have been happenin' tonight. If you ride with us you may get clear of town.'

Kirk shook his head. 'I've got work to do here,' he said thinly. 'Culver is in town and his foreman, Fleck. I've got a score to settle with them.'

'What chance do you reckon you'll have if you stay here?'

Kirk shrugged, aware that Emmy was watching him too, knowing that she wanted him to change his mind and ride out with them to the Manson spread where there would be a certain amount of safety for him. But he shook his head again. 'If you can get this hombre to Manson, he'll know how to make him talk. Once the other ranchers learn of this, they may decide to forget their fears of each other and band together. It will be the only chance they have of saving themselves from Culver. If you can get them to ride into town with their men, we may finish him while he's here, away from the Double Lance.'

Herdson pondered that for a few moments, turning it over in his mind, still obviously doubtful. Then he nodded finally. 'You're takin' a big chance,' he acknowledged. 'But I guess you could be right. It's the only way. I've still got some friends among the ranchers in this territory and even though we can't rely on Cantry and his deputies, we may be able to force a showdown in which they'll have to come in on our side.'

Moving across the room, he took down a polished Winchester from the wall, thrust shells into it, then nodded towards Telfer. 'Better get movin',' he said grimly. 'And don't get any ideas about makin' a run for it because I'm an old man. There won't be any Culver's men watching the trail I mean to take out of town. I know this place far better than he does.'

For a moment, Kirk felt a faint sense of uneasiness in his mind at letting the older man take all of the responsibility of getting a dangerous gunman such as Telfer out of town and across those miles of open range, but he pushed the thought quickly from his mind as he realised he had no other choice. His own position would be extremely precarious and his life might depend on what Herdson could do to persuade the other ranchers to throw in their forces behind him and Manson and ride on Wasatch.

'I'll go with Father,' said Emmy, as he turned his glance on her. She gave a faint smile as she noticed the look on his face. 'Don't worry. I can handle a gun just as well as a man. And—' Here she paused, and looked towards Telfer, 'it won't take much for me to shoot this killer in the back if he makes any funny moves.'

The moon was high as Kirk made his way slowly back towards the middle of town. It cast a pale white radiance over everything, forming vague, moving shadows which attracted his attention continually, although he knew that there was nothing there, as yet, to present any danger to him. The firing which he had heard an hour or so earlier, concentrated to the west of the town, had died away almost completely and the houses lay in dark silence on either side of him.

At any moment he expected to hear more gunfire break out but the minutes passed and there was nothing to break the silence except for the quiet sounds of his feet in the dirt. Moving Indian-like through the stillness, he approached a narrow alley that drifted away in midnight darkness in the direction of the main street. It was well after midnight now, somewhere in the early hours of the morning, yet as he reached the alley mouth and peered into the moonlit greyness of the main street, he saw that there were yellow lights in the windows of two of the saloons and that one light still shone on the upper floor of the hotel. Outside, there were several horses, tethered to the hitching rails and a quick glance told him that they were Double Lance mounts. He let his keen gaze move along the whole length of the street. Culver was evidently still in town, with most of his men and Kirk's plan depended on keeping them here for as long as possible.

The doors of the nearer saloon swung open, as he pressed himself close into the wall. Two men staggered outside. They had their arms around each other's shoulders in the usual attitude of drunken men, almost fell as they tried to walk down the wooden steps to the street. Pausing for a moment, they sank down on the edge of the boardwalk, each taking a swig from the bottle.

Kirk paused for a moment and when no one else came from the saloon, he guessed these men had been ordered to watch the street and keep guard over the horses. Certainly one way of keeping the riders in town for the rest of the night would be to run off their horses and a quick glance was enough to tell him that if he could get across the street without being seen by either of those two men he stood a good chance of doing that.

Bending low, he edged back into the alley, moved over to the other side and slipped up on to the shadowed boardwalk, moving catlike along the front of the store. Reaching the far end, he edged forward into the street. Here, there were few shadows, with the high moon flooding the street with light, but the two men some fifty yards away were too engrossed in finishing the bottle of whiskey to turn and keep a close watch on what was happening around them.

It took him almost a full minute to reach the other side of the street and crawl along the boardwalk until he was at the corner of the saloon, for even though the two men were drunk he could not afford to make so much as one little discordant sound. The night was entirely hushed now that the firing had died away and he eased himself down beneath the rail very slowly. The two men sat with their backs to him less than ten feet away, muttering drunkenly. The bottle seemed to be almost finished. Slipping one of the Colts soundlessly from its holster, he reversed it, gripping it tightly by the barrel. Everything would have to be done with the minimum of sound now, otherwise he might warn the rest of the men inside the saloon. He could just pick out the intermittent sound of voices beyond the swing doors. Thrusting his feet under him, he hung there, poised for a moment, eyes on the two men just below him. Then he moved swiftly and without warning. One of the men was on the point of rising to his feet, the empty bottle in his hand, intent on returning to the saloon for another, when the butt of the pistol in Kirk's hand connected savagely with the side of his head. He collapsed without a sound into the dust and the gun was already moving in a downward arc towards the unprotected head of the other man by the time he hit the ground.

Raising himself a little, he paused outside the swing doors, just able to glance inside. All of the lanterns had been lit, and the crystal mirror behind the bar reflected light into the room. Most of the men were standing at the bar, drinking, and he felt a sudden tightness come to his chest muscles as he recognised one of them, even though the man's back was towards him. Culver had not changed too much during the past ten years. He was more prosperous-looking, wore far better clothing than he had when Kirk had known him earlier, but his features were still the same, having coarsened just a little. It would have been so easy to lift his gun and shoot the other down there and then; and it was only by an effort of will that he fought down the impulse. He wanted Culver to know who it was who had shot him, not to die with a bullet in his back and not know who had sent him into eternity, or why.

Turning away, he went down the wooden steps, ignoring the two unconscious men at the bottom. Making his way along the line of horses, he untied the ropes and bridles quickly. For a moment, the animals milled aimlessly in the dusty street. Then, backing away from in front of the saloon, he fired a single shot into the air. The din was deafening, the effect on the horses just what Kirk had expected. Within seconds, they were stampeding along the street, kicking up a cloud of dust that hung greyly in the moonshine.

Scarcely a moment passed before the doors of both saloons swung open and a crowd of men spilled into the street, many with their guns drawn, glinting bluely in the moonlight. Culver was there, thrusting himself to the fore-front of the men. He yelled harshly: 'It must have been Brennan. He's cut loose the horses and spooked 'em. Spread out, boys, and find him. There's a couple of hundred dollars for the man who brings him in, dead or alive.'

Kirk backed off sharply. Things were liable to get tough within a few moments but at least he had done what he had set out to do, made it impossible for these men to get out of town that night. When the riderless horses turned up at the Double Lance ranch, somebody would get suspicious and ride into town to see what had happened.

This time, he had checked the alley that stretched away at his back, knew exactly where it led and moved swiftly along it. The pressure of the men rushing along the main street passed over the mouth of the alley and a small group of them swung into it, running quickly in a tightly-bunched cluster of bodies. Every muscle in his body was so tight that his flesh began to ache; and there were sharp stabbing pangs of cramp in his thighs as he slid over a low wall and crouched down, listening to the thump of heavy feet on the hard ground. He had a creepy feeling in his mind, and there was a brief moment of utter panic as the men stopped almost directly opposite the spot where he lay. He lay quite still, scarcely daring to breathe, keeping well down, knowing that the gunhawks were less than a foot from him, searching around with eyes and ears for any sign of him. There was a sudden burst of fire. A man grunted something inaudible nearby and the men ran on. Lying there, he followed the shift of gunfire as it began to swing around. The men were drunk, were firing at shadows, hoping to hit him if they fired enough shots into the dark corners and through the flimsy wood of the empty buildings that lined the intersecting alleys.

Culver would not rest until he had found him and knew he was dead. Sooner or later, he meant to wipe out every man who opposed him, but he wanted Kirk Brennan more than any of the others. He would search every single corner of Wasatch for him, break down every door and send slugs into every black shadow in search of him.

In his mind's eye there was a clear picture of the ground around him and rising to his hands and knees, he crawled forward alongside the wall. His hands found a part where it was splintered and broken and he paused for a moment, then lifted his head to stare into the dark alley. It was empty in both directions. The men had heard the firing, had thought it meant he had been cornered somewhere and not wishing to miss the fun, had moved on without carrying out a thorough search. Cautiously, he drew himself up to his full height, expecting to hear the bark of a gun and feel the smashing, leaden impact of a slug in his body.

Nothing happened. Flattened to the wall, he waited again, holding his breath until it hurt in his chest. Nobody seemed to be watching this alley now and in a moment, he had reached the far end, where it joined another one at right angles. He put his head cautiously around the sharply-angled corner, seeing nothing at all in the moon-curdled shadows of the alley running between the backs of the houses and the adjoining warehouses. Drawing in his breath sharply, he stepped out into the open, crowded close to the wall on the far side of the alley and remained there for a few moments, listening to the yelling of men and the occasional sound of a gun blast.

He had left the most dangerous spot in the town; he had moved away from it and out into the loose darkness. Softly, he let his breath fall away in small pinches of sound, crept to the rear end of the alley, away from the main street and the saloons.

All around him it seemed, completely at random, the shouting went on as the wolf pack of men scoured the town for him. A man came out of the black shadows some twenty yards away, paused as he crossed the alley where the moonlight touched him with its pale, cold radiance, then ran quickly past, his breath snorting in his mouth. As soon as he had gone, Kirk ran across the passage in front of him, moved towards the large storehouse which loomed high over the other buildings clustered around it.

Whatever happened, he had to get off the street. If he didn't sooner or later, someone was going to be lucky and find him and a single warning cry would bring the whole weight of the Double Lance crew down on him. He half expected to find some of the gunhawks in the place, but there was nothing there, except for a rat that scurried across the floor, paused in one corner, in a patch of moonlight, and glared balefully at him from red eyes.

Glancing to his left and right, he discovered nothing. The place was empty. In one corner, he noticed several bales of hay, but except for these, the bottom floor of the building was empty.

Letting his weight fall easy and slow, he moved forward, feeling in front of him as he went until his hand touched something hard and unyielding. It was cold under his touch, slanted upward at an angle. His fingers explored it further and he found that it was the stairway leading upward. Sliding his hand over one of the steps, he leaned downward with all of his weight, found that it would take his bulk and laid his feet on the steps. They creaked and groaned ominously, but bore his weight. He went up slowly, body flattened as he climbed.

Two minutes later, his hands touched the second floor's level and he pulled himself forward gently. Around him was the fathomless black. No moonlight shone in through the opening in the slanting roof although he could make out several bright stars glittering in the heavens.

In the screening blackness, he stretched himself out on the thick layer of straw near the opening. The night wind blew coldly in, swirling around his body and he pulled his jacket collar up more tightly around his neck. He could have moved further back into the room, but from here it was possible to look down over the rabbit-warren of narrow alleys through which the gunhawks of the Double Lance would come. At least, he could have warning of their presence, but at the moment they seemed to be some distance away, on the far edge of town.

When the firing and shouting showed no tendency to come any closer, he hunted around in the dimness, found a tattered old blanket, and wrapped it around him, huddling down on the straw, legs under him, seeking what little warmth he could get. His face was sticky with sweat and when he pulled off his hat for a moment, his hair was plastered down against his scalp and drops of sweat fell from his forehead and tasted salt on his lips. Hunger twisted in his belly but there was no chance of getting anything to eat and he was forced to let his stomach growl. He felt weary too and there was a continuing ache in his chest which did not let up. Lying back, he thought about Herdson and Emmy. Had they succeeded in reaching Manson's place without trouble? In spite of the old man's confident insistence that he knew a way out of Wasatch which would not be watched by Culver's men, Kirk felt a growing sense of unease in his mind. They were playing a dangerous game here and for very high stakes. By now, Culver would have realised what he was up against and the strength of the opposition which faced him and he would lay his plans accordingly. The spooking of the horses would be the one thing he would not expect, but it would tend to show him something of what was in Kirk's mind.

Rubbing the growth of beard on his chin, he pondered on what might be in Culver's mind. The other would know that he had slipped through the net which had been spread for him once before, and would possibly know that Telfer was missing. The chances were that he might send most of his men out to reinforce those watching the roads out of town, determined to ensure that whatever else happened, he did not leave Wasatch. Then it would be a comparatively simple thing to hunt him down at first light. He realised that the shouting had died down in the distance and debated the reason for this in his mind, finally deciding that Culver may have called in the rest of his men once he was satisfied there was no way of escape for him from town. It made some sort of sense. The other would not want to lose more of his men, being shot from ambush in the moonlight. He would wait until it was light and he could get Cantry to join him in the search.

With this thought in his mind, he sank back on to the straw, stretching his legs out in front of him. He had no great difficulty in keeping awake. Like most range men he needed very little sleep and the thought that some of Culver's men might try to sneak up on him through the night and take him by surprise was an added incentive towards remaining alert through the small hours of the morning. He drowsed occasionally, as the night passed slowly and the moon dipped further to the west, but the slightest sound was enough to bring him swiftly awake, jerking upright and peering about him. Deep in the chilly blackness that preceded the grey dawn, he rolled himself a cigarette and lit it cautiously, checking that there was no one in sight outside, and keeping his head well back from the opening. A sharp-eyed marksman could spot the faint red glow of a lighted cigarette a mile away and draw a bead on it within seconds. He smoked the cigarette through and tried to rest, staring out into the velvet blackness, watchfully awaiting the first steely grey streaks of light which would mark the coming of the dawn. The air was cold and damp now and beyond the store, the buildings formed loose outlines which, as the shadows began to grow progressively lighter took on form and substance.

When the brightening new warmth of the fresh dawn came flooding in over the distant hills, touching the roofs of the buildings that made up Wasatch, Kirk stirred, looked down from the opening. He could just see where the main street cut across the town, but the houses on this side made it impossible for him to see anybody who might be abroad at that moment, except for two places where narrow alleys cut into the street and afforded him a brief view. Soon, the whole town would be awake, looking for him.

Stepping to the opening, he tried to catch a glance of the alleys far to his right but found that his field of vision was too limited. The next moment, a sudden movement below made him pull back sharply. The man had stepped out of a narrow opening, into the small square less than three hundred yards away and now he was peering about him intently. Lifting his gaze a little, Kirk saw more men moving with a slow deliberateness among the buildings. He counted ten of them, spaced out and moving with caution; and although it was still not full daylight, he was able to recognise the bulky figure of Fleck, the Double Lance foreman, in the lead.

He fingered the Colt for a moment, knew that the men were out of killing range of a revolver and lowered his arm slowly. There was no sense in giving away his position for

133

nothing. The men began to move in closer, ringing him round. This time there was a singleness of purpose in their movements which contrasted sharply with the way they had acted during the night. He guessed that many of them had had a chance to sober up and that Culver had given strict orders that he was to be found – and fast. Culver would soon be running out of patience and his men would have to pay for it.

There was a clear shout from somewhere below him, echoing among the buildings and glancing down, Kirk was in time to see one of the men pointing up at the top of the storehouse where he was hidden. He doubted if the other had seen him. More likely it was that this was one place they had not yet searched and the other was yelling to the men to move in and go over the place.

Fleck took up the shout, motioning the men forward in a wide circle. Kirk sucked air down into his lung, checked the chambers of his sixguns. He could take some of those men with him, but no man could kill them all. And there were probably two or three dozen more scattered around town, not counting those that Cantry could bring up, ready to come running once gunfire broke out.

'Send in a few shots,' yelled Fleck from down below. ' If he's in there, we should be able to force him out without risking anybody goin' up after him.'

The men on the ground were taking no chances. Crouching behind the low walls, they pumped shots methodically through the flimsy wooden walls of the building. Kirk lay flat on the floor, listening to the crackle of the slugs as they tore through the wood. Lead came in through the planks near him in short, gusty snorts of sound and one or two crashed through the floor of the loft within inches of his prone body.

The firing ceased for a moment and Kirk lay there, fast-thinking. The men were probably taking time to reload, to improve their positions, and all the time, the daylight was brightening and the shadows were paling in the alleys. Very gently, he eased himself forward, risked a quick look down into the open space which fronted the building. A man yelled harshly and out of the corner of his eye, Kirk saw the other lift his rifle and send a shot crashing through the opening, the lead scorching past his cheek like an angry inset. Aiming and squeezing the trigger in a single movement, he dropped the man in his tracks. The slug hit the man low in the belly, smashing through the abdomen, destroying the nerve system, paralysing the other. He slumped to his knees, then pitched forward and in the same moment, Fleck yelled: 'Keep him pinned down men and we'll soon have him out of there.'

Gritting his teeth, Kirk looked about him desperately for some way out of the storehouse. It seemed impossible. They would have sent men to cover the rear and he had no way of forcing the men below out of range. Then his eye fell on the large bales of dry straw near the wall. A sudden wild idea entered his mind. It offered him a very slender chance, one that was virtually impossibly remote, but it was the only one he had.

Taking the box of sulphur matches from his pocket, he inched forward until he reached the nearest bale. The breeze was blowing in through the opening and this was going to make things doubly difficult and dangerous for him, but there was no other way out. Striking one of the matches, he applied the flame to the bottom of the bale. The flames caught instantly, crackling through the dry straw, fanned backward by the stiff breeze, licking out towards his face. The heat singed his hair and burned his flesh as he moved quickly back. More firing broke out from below and there was a confused yelling immediately below the opening.

Waiting until the flames were leaping several feet into the air, Kirk kicked strongly at the blazing bale. For a moment, it resisted him, then it slid forward, teetered on the lip of the opening for a second, before plummeting down to the ground below. There was no time for the men there to get out of the way. They had considered themselves to be safe so long as they remained close to the wall of the building, knowing that he dared not expose himself to the fire of their companions behind the nearby walls, to shoot down on them. This belief proved to be their undoing. The blazing straw showered on top of them, trapping several against the wall. Kirk listened to the yells and screams for a moment before moving over to another of the bales, dragging it to the edge of the opening, before firing it. Heat struck forcibly at him, burning his face as the wind carried the sparks and flames back into the loft. Kicking it out, he drew back, then pulled himself upright, edged to the wall on one side of the opening and peered out. Men were running in all directions down below, scurrying like ants when boiling water is poured on to their anthill. Some had smouldering clothes on their bodies. One man, shrieking harshly, dived headlong into a horse-trough, splashing the water in all directions. A volley of rifle fire crashed up at him from the rest of the men, forcing him to pull his head back.

Smoke caught at the back of his nostrils and a faint crackling sound caused him to whirl sharply. Flames were licking along the back of the loft where sparks had caught at the straw on the floor, setting it instantly alight.

Kirk waited to see no more. The immediate danger was now to him. He had to get to the trapdoor and down into the lower part of the building before the leaping flames gained a firmer hold and cut off his escape. The fire had spread rapidly through straw as dry as tinder and one of the larger bales was already burning fiercely in one corner. Coughing as the smoke swirled about him, thick and irritating, he staggered towards the trapdoor, tears blinding him. Tiny flickers of red-tongued flame spurted up around his feet as he struggled with the slippery, smoul-

136

dering straw underfoot, came to a full pause at the edge of the trapdoor to gain his balance, and then lowered himself slowly over the edge and on to the topmost rung of the ladder. It swayed precariously under him as he worked his way down it. Gaining the lower floor, he stood for a long moment, looking about him. Smoke was already beginning to billow down through the opening in the ceiling and there was more coming in through the door of the storehouse. Outside, through the confused shouting, he heard Fleck yelling more orders, trying to urge the men into the building. It was evident that none of them wanted to go inside. They must already have been aware that the roof was ablaze and that it might fall in and collapse on them at any moment if they should venture inside. Tying his neckpiece across his mouth and nostrils, Kirk moved silently in the direction of the door, both Colts balanced in his fists, fingers tight on the triggers. His vision was blurred by the smoke and even as he reached the door, a section of the ceiling came crashing down into the lower room in a splintering of blazing timbers. He stood for a moment at the door, remembering the layout of the alleys outside, the whereabouts of the main body of men as he had seen them from the upper storey. Presently, this whole building would be a mass of flames. Nothing could put out his blaze now

Jerking up the guns, he leapt out into the open, flung himself bodily sideways in anticipation of a shot. The big Colts were already belching lead while he was in mid-air, in an almost horizontal position. He had a vague impression of men milling around, their smouldering clothing burning brightly as they fanned the flames with their own violent movements, and his first slug took one of the men high in the chest, hurling him backward under the slamming impact. Another man, swinging sharply, lowering his gaze in stunned surprise, tried to jerk his gun around, to bring it to bear on Kirk as he hit the ground and wriggled swiftly sideways towards the corner of the building. Kirk loosed off a couple of shots at the other and the man dropped his gun in a stupid fashion, the slug tearing into the ground at his feet as his finger squeezed the trigger in the last motion of life. He stood there for a moment, his knees gently buckling under him as if no longer able to bear his weight, the red blood pumping from his open mouth and trickling down his chin with every exhalation.

He was ten feet from the corner of the building before the men collected their scattered wits. The blazing bundles of straw which had dropped among them had paralysed their thinking, had taken them utterly by surprise. It took them several moments to collect their wits and by the time they did so, two more men had been hit as they tried to run forward, collapsing over the bodies of the men already slain and Kirk was out of sight around the corner of the building, running swiftly for the rear.

Just as he reached the far corner, a man came blundering at him. A tall, square-shouldered man, his face battle-scarred, with a deep cut across his forehead where a bullet had probably creased the skin, glancing off the bone. There was no time to think, and Kirk thumbed back the hammers of his guns the moment he saw the other, the movements swift and instinctive.

The gunman's right hand darted for the gun at his waist. It was clear from the frozen look on his features that Kirk was the last person he had expected to see. His gun was half drawn from leather when the weapon in Kirk's right hand spoke. The heavy .45 slug struck the other just below the breastbone, knocking him sideways so that his shoulders struck the wall of the building and he slid slowly down it, knees bending under him, his legs sliding out. Kirk stepped over them without paying the dead man a second glance. There was the harsh babble of voices at his back, coming closer. The sound of running men angling around the tall building, sounding above the fierce crackle of flames as they took an even firmer hold on the dry wood and straw inside.

There was no one visible at the back of the building. In front of him, a double line of dirty shacks, broken, dusty windows faintly glinting in the sunlight, stretched away on either side of an alley that ran straight as a die for more than two hundred yards. It was the only way out and he knew he had to take it. Hurling himself forward, he ran along it, feet pounding in the dirt, the breath rasping harshly in his lungs, his heart pounding in his chest. He knew the gunmen, with Dan Fleck in their lead could not be far behind him now, knew that it was virtually impossible for him to cover those two hundred yards before they reached the end of the alley and began firing after him.

He was more than halfway along the alley before a shout told him that he had been seen. What to do now? Stop and fire, try to keep them busy and move back a step at a time – or run on and risk being shot in the back? It was one of those snap decisions which had to be taken without a pause in which to think things out and which could mean life or death.

He continued to run, feet slipping in the dust. A solitary shot came after him, ricocheting off the wall. Then there was a lull before another shot followed. Something plucked at the sleeve of his jacket, burned along his arm. Then he broke his stride as a small group of men appeared at the end of the alley directly in front of him, blocking off that avenue of escape. He lifted both Colts to fire on the run, then relaxed the pressure on the triggers as he recognised the grizzled features of Laredo and behind him, more of the Manson crew.

Ducking his head, he ran towards them. Even as he drew level with them, they began pumping shots into the Double Lance men running along the alley less than seventy yards away. It flashed through Kirk's mind that they were still heavily outnumbered by the others, but at

139

the moment, as things were, they held the advantage. Swinging round, he fired at the gunhawks, aiming low. A man fell, bringing down three men close behind him, blocking the alley for those at the back. Caught in the savage crossfire, they struggled to turn and run back in the direction from which they had just come.

'Keep firin' at the critters,' yelled Laredo thinly. He aimed and fired in the same movement as the Double Lance men retreated, dragging their wounded with them, sending an occasional shot along the alley. One of the men near Kirk staggered as a bullet struck him in the thigh and he went down, striking Kirk heavily as he fell.

Glancing down, Kirk hauled the other out of the line of fire, settled him with his back against the dusty stone wall. The man's face was twisted with pain and glistening with sweat as he held his leg, bending it at the knee, thrusting it almost clear to his chest.

'Don't hold the wound like that,' he told the man sharply. 'Grab your leg higher, squeeze tightly. That way, you'll stop the bleedin' until we can get a doctor to you.' He lifted his head, stared up at Laredo. 'Is there any doctor who'll defy Culver and come to take a look at him?'

'Doc Winters might,' said the other harshly. 'He's an old man and nobody cares much about him. I'll get one of the men to fetch him.' He turned to the man at his back and snapped an order. The other hesitated for a moment and then moved off.

'Just lie still and quit moving around,' Laredo said thinly to the wounded man. 'If you keep jerking about like that, you'll start it bleedin' again.'

'It feels like a red-hot bar thrust into my leg,' said the other through tightly-clenched teeth. He rocked back and forth with the agony of the wound, eyes closed tightly, face twisted into a grimace. 'You reckon I'll lose my leg because of this?' There was a trace of fear in his voice.

'The doctor will take a look at you when he gets here,'

Laredo snapped. 'Now just sit back and keep quiet. Those hombres will be tryin' to work their way around us soon. At the moment, there aren't enough of us to hold 'em off if they do hit us in force.'

'Where were you all durin' the night?' Kirk asked harshly. 'They had me holed up twice.'

'We heard the shootin', but there was nothin' to tell us who was bein' hunted down, although I reckon we should have guessed it might have been you.' There was a faint, vague note of apology in his tone. 'I suppose you were the one who stampeded all of their horses out of town.'

'That's right. I caught up with that coyote named Telfer. He tried to take me in one of the churches. I got him to Herdson and he and his daughter were tryin' to get him to Manson through the night.'

'To Manson! They'd never make it. From what we learned, every trail out of here was watched by some of Culver's men.'

'Herdson was pretty certain he knew a way of slipping out without bein' seen. I didn't stop to ask him which it was. But if they do manage to get through, I'm hopin' they can talk some of the other ranchers into bringin' their men here and forcin' a showdown with Culver now that we have him trapped in town.'

# CHAPTER SEVEN

# RANGE JUSTICE

Kirk removed his hat, feeling it sticking to his forehead. The sun had now lifted clear of the horizon and already the shadows were shortening in the alleys. So far, Culver and his men had made no attempt to rush them, although their defensive position was far from adequate. Kirk glanced about him. They had pulled back from their former position and were now crouched down on the outskirts of the town, with their backs to the house which belonged to Herdson. Two of the wounded men had been carried inside, where they would be comparatively safe and Doc Winters was, at that very moment, tending to their wounds.

Glancing round at Laredo, he saw the faint smile that formed on the oldster's lips, the bright gleam at the back of his narrowed eyes as he squinted up at the sun. Sucking in his cheeks, he said quietly: 'It's goin' to be a hot day, Kirk. I'm thinkin' that Culver's men won't want to be lyin' out there in the blisterin' heat any longer than they can help. They'll rush us just as soon as they figure they've got enough men to swamp us in the first attack.'

Kirk nodded, pressing his lips tightly together. He replaced the hat on his head, clamping it down firmly over

142

his scalp, threw a quick glance behind him out beyond the house which stood some fifty yards away. 'I'm more worried about those men he has watchin' the trail,' he mused.

The other allowed a gust of expression to pass over his grizzled face. He spat a plug of chewed tobacco into the dirt, propped himself up on one elbow and asked, 'You figure they may try to stop the rest of the boys gettin' into town in a hurry?'

'Nope. I figure somebody may get through to them and tell them to ride in and hit us from the rear. If we're pinned down between two lines of fire we don't have much of a chance, even if we get into the house.'

'You've got a point there, I reckon,' nodded the other. He held Kirk's glance silently for a moment, then swung his head round sharply as gunfire lashed them from one of the houses twenty yards away. The glass in one of the upper windows was shattered suddenly and out of the corner of his eye, Kirk saw the smooth, shining barrel of a rifle pointed out, turning in their direction. He lifted his arm and fired instinctively, saw the rifle pulled back sharply as his bullet struck flesh, heard the man give up a loud cry as he staggered back into the room. Muzzle flashes showed from the windows of the nearby house. Bullets screeched and sang as they ricocheted off the walls. So long as the men kept their heads well down the walls afforded them good cover except from the men in the upper windows.

A minute passed; and then the firing died down abruptly. Kirk settled down beside Laredo to wait. He could feel the tension beginning to pile up, like the heat and the stillness just before a desert storm.

'Laredo!'

The oldster jerked his head up suddenly at the unexpected sound of his name from one of the nearby buildings.

Kirk held a tight grip on the other's arm. He knew it had been Fleck, even though he could not see the foreman. 'Don't answer him,' he hissed softly.

After a brief pause Fleck went on: 'I know it's you and some of the Manson crew out there, Laredo. You've got no call to fight us. We don't want to kill any of you. We're only interested in one man you've got with you. Turn him over to us and you're all free to ride on out of town unmolested.'

Laredo said nothing. Out of the corner of his vision, Kirk could see a tiny muscle twitching high in the other's cheek, but apart from that he had given no outward sign of any emotion.

'Don't be a goshdarned fool,' came Fleck's voice once more. 'We've got you completely surrounded. You've no hope of gettin' away and once we come in it will mean the finish of you. Do you reckon that's what Manson wants, to lose all of his hands, just to save the life of one man who means nothin' whatever to you. Even if you've got some sense of misguided loyalty to this man, ask the rest of your crew if they want to die for him. Go ahead – see what they say about it.'

Thinning his lips, Laredo could stand it no longer. He yelled harshly. 'You aren't tellin' us what to do, Fleck. We don't take orders from you. As for not havin' a chance, I reckon the tables will be turned pretty soon and that's what is worryin' you now. You know you can't get out of town without your horses.'

There was a longer pause. It was almost as if the foreman were debating with someone else. Then Culver's voice sounded. Kirk felt a growing tightness under his ribs as the other called. 'What's Brennan to you, Laredo? He's just a two-bit killer, still wanted by the law for rustlin' and murder. Old Man Herdson knows about it. Sheriff Cantry still has the wanted posters for him and the reward is still payable to anyone who brings him in, dead or alive. Is that the sort of man you want to give your lives for?' There was a note of scorn in the other's voice.

Not lifting his head, Kirk called: 'These men know what you are, Culver. And as soon as Manson gets through with your man, Telfer, everyone in Wasatch will know that it was you rustled Herdson's cattle ten years ago and shot that man on the trail. You don't have much time left now. Pretty soon, Herdson will be back with more men than you have to back you.'

'Don't listen to him,' called Culver tightly. Kirk tried to place the other man's voice as he went on: 'Herdson is just a crazy old fool who never forgave me for bein' a better business man and rancher than he was. As for a man called Telfer, I've never heard the name and he certainly hasn't been on my payroll. This is just another of Brennan's lies to get you to back him.'

'Can you see where he is?' Laredo asked in a tight whisper.

Kirk lifted his head a couple of inches, then shook it slowly. 'He's back there among those houses someplace,' he said, exhaling quietly. 'But he won't be showing himself to us unless he can help it. He has his men to fight and die for him.'

Laredo gave a vicious grin, lifted his revolver, aimed it swiftly at one of the sun bright windows and squeezed off a solitary shot. The glass vanished in shards of light as the bullet struck home. For a moment, it was as if the slug had had no other effect. Then a body appeared in the shattered opening, hung there limply for a second before pitching crazily into the alley below.

'Figured I saw some skunk moving at the back of that glass,' observed Laredo harshly.

The shot brought a savage burst of return fire from the hidden outlaws. The din was deafening and from it Kirk judged that the Double Lance men had formed a wide arc around their position, hemming them in on three sides. If

145

they succeeded in working their way any closer, they would be able to fire right across the path he and the others would have to take to get back to the house. They would be forced to run a savage gauntlet of fire before they reached the comparative safety of Herdson's place.

The situation was rapidly getting more dangerous, yet he knew that they had to hold off Culver's men for as long as possible out there. Once they were made to retreat to the house, the outlaws would have excellent cover from which to pour a deadly hail of fire into the building and thick and strong as the walls were, they would not hold off that sort of fire for long.

Wriggling forward, Kirk edged to the fullest extent of their shielding wall, keeping his head well down, risking a quick glance around it, took a long sighting with his Colt and fired. The bullet struck less than an inch from where a rifle barrel protruded from the half-open doorway of the building directly opposite them. He saw the gun barrel waver, then withdraw with a jerk as the outlaw flinched, yanking it out of sight.

One of the Manson crew, shot high in the shoulder, was propped against the wall a couple of yards away. He craned his neck to try to see how badly he had been hurt and the movement, slight as it was, brought a murderous hail of slugs against the wall. Pieces of stone struck Kirk on the face as he pulled himself down, huddled on his stomach.

Thumbing shells into his sixgun, he stared around the corner of the wall again, saw the rush of men who came pouring through the doorway of a building a little further along the alley. Swiftly, he signalled to Laredo, saw the other give a quick nod, motion to the rest of the men. The outlaws' plan was obvious. While the men in the upper windows gave covering fire, the others intended to rush them.

He fired swiftly and instinctively, scarcely pausing to

146

take aim. Bullets sang and chirruped about him and the trapped echoes bounced off the brick and wood, hammering at his ears. Two of the running men slithered forward, tilting on to their faces as they were gunshot, weapons falling from hands no longer having life in them to retain their grip. The others hesitated and this proved to be their undoing. Caught in a vicious cross fire from the Manson crew, they had no chance at all.

They began running back for cover, with Fleck's bull-like voice roaring at them to keep moving forward. Pressing his shoulder hard against the wall, Kirk continued to fire until the hammer clicked on an empty chamber, then pulled himself back alongside Laredo.

The situation was rapidly becoming desperate as more of the Double Lance men, keeping well under cover, began crawling forward on three sides. The frontal assault on their position had been a feint; he realised that now and cursed himself for not having seen it before. Having to concentrate most of their defensive fire on the men moving up directly in front of them, had given the others their chance to swing around and crowd in on them from the flanks.

'We've got to get back to the house or we'll be cut off entirely,' he said thinly. 'Warn the others.'

A sudden silence came. One of those oddly inexplicable lulls in the middle of a gunfight. Kirk smelled danger in the stillness, but it was the best chance they were going to get. It might be that the others were busy reloading. Whatever the reason, he waved the men to move back to the house. Two of them reached down and grabbed the man with the shoulder wound, carrying him between them. Sobbing groans of agony came from between his lips as the jolting motion sent stabs of pain through his body, but the two bearers gave no sign of hearing, but continued to run, stumbling under the dead weight. Kirk lay flat on his stomach for a long moment, eyes watching the houses around them, ready to cover the others.

It was a reckless chance, but it paid off. Only half a dozen shots followed them as they pulled back towards the house. Even though he must surely have been expecting such a move, it appeared to have taken Culver completely by surprise.

Not until he and Laredo crowded inside the door, slamming it shut behind them did a volley of gunfire crash out from the outlaws' positions. Moving to one side of the windows, he crouched down, staring out into the flooding sunlight, thankful that the house lay so far from the main street and the other buildings. It meant the others would have to cross that wide stretch of open ground before they got to them. His eyes moved over the ground in front of the building, then lifted to the houses in the distance. An occasional flash of red showed in one of the windows and a rifle bullet would strike close to the house, kicking up a sharp puff of dust.

'They won't risk their skins until they've drawn most of our fire,' Laredo said from the other window. 'They know we can't make a move now without them seein' it.'

Kirk nodded. 'I reckon this is as good a place as any for us.' He turned as the white-haired figure appeared in the doorway. 'How are the wounded men, Doc?'

Winters came into the room, keeping well clear of the line of fire through the windows. Evidently he had been in a position similar to this before, Kirk thought. 'They'll live, I reckon,' he said eventually. He wrinkled his brows in a sudden frown. 'I hope you've been considering how we're to get out of here. From what I can see, Culver has got this place completely surrounded now and he has far more men to back his play than you have. They can afford to wait until it's dark and then rush you.'

Kirk shook his head emphatically. 'They can't, Doc,' he said quietly. 'They know that time is on our side, not theirs.'

148

Doc Winters looked perplexed. He said: 'How do you figure that, Brennan?'

'We've got one of his men out at Manson's place right now. Herdson and Emmy smuggled him out of town through the night. By now, they'll have made him talk, and I reckon that after some of the smaller ranchers hear what he has to say, they'll come ridin' this way with as many men as they can spare to put an end to Matt Culver once and for all.'

The other's bushy white brows lifted in an expression of surprise. 'Are you sure that Herdson got out of town safely? Seems to me that Culver had plenty of men watching the trails out. I doubt if a dog could've slipped past his men last night.'

Kirk said firmly: 'I'm banking on him anyway, Doc. He's got to have gotten through.' There was a sinking feeling in his mind as he realised that the other could be right. Herdson had seemed so sure that he knew a way out of town that was not watched, yet he might have been wrong and at this very moment, Culver would be gloating to himself, letting them think that they had got away with it, knowing all the while that they had no chance of being reinforced. It was something he did not wish to think about at that moment and thrust the idea out of his mind.

From the sounds of distant gunfire outside, it struck him that Culver was moving his men up so that they were within range of sixgun fire. The rifles were all right for long distance firing, and were probably far more accurate than the Colts, but they would not be able to send in such a withering hail of fire as the hand guns and it would be Culver's intent to saturate the walls and windows of the building with lead.

'Some of 'em movin' up yonder,' said Laredo tightly. He jerked a thumb in the direction of the main street.

Carefully, Kirk lifted his head, peered over the ledge of the window. In the harsh glare of sunlight, he could make out the figures running from one concealing shadow to another, holding themselves low, sometimes firing from the hip as they ran. They were using sixguns and the range was at the very extreme for these weapons and the danger from these men was not so much from their present fire as from the fact that they would soon be able to reach a position where they could cover the rest of their men while they moved up in turn. These were the tactics used in the Civil War to such good effect and it seemed highly likely that they might be equally successful here.

He brought up his Colt, lined the sights on one of the men, nearer than the others, waited for the man to climb to his feet once more, ready to run forward. When he did so, there was perhaps two seconds for Kirk to take final aim and fire. Squeezing off the shot, he saw the man continue to lunge forward and guessed that his shot had missed. Then he saw the other swing round, throw up his arms over his head as if trying to clutch at something invisible in the air above him, and drop on to his face. He had been able to catch only a momentary glimpse of the other's face, but it had been enough for him to confirm what he had half-suspected. It had been Dan Fleck, the Double Lance foreman. Now he lay stretched out in the blazing hot sunlight, legs twisted under him, unmoving.

A full volley crashed against the side of the house, shaking the wall and sending a shower of glass splinters into the room as the window was smashed. Kirk dropped to the floor behind the window and heard the savage splitting of wood immediately above him as more bullets tore into the window ledge. A raw splinter, cutting downward, struck him in the back of the hand and  he instinctively flinched away, rolling on to his side. Feeling for the long splinter, he pulled it out, felt the warm gush of blood flowing over his hand and pulled his neckpiece from around his throat, winding it tightly around his hand, closing his fingers on it. The main weight of fire still seemed to be pressing against this side of the house, although he guessed that there would be men moving around them, hoping to find some side unprotected. More slugs beat through the air above his head, flattened themselves into the wall of the other side of the room.

Drawing his breath, he pushed his back hard against the wall and sat there for a long moment, focusing his eyes on the rest of the men around him. His mind was very clear and abnormally sharp and he seemed to be able to hear every tiny sound as if it were curiously magnified. He was able to follow the firing as it now began to work itself around the house as more of Culver's men moved up into position.

He drew himself slowly upward, checked his guns and laid his full weight on both feet, beginning an inching progress that carried him to the side of the shattered window. Glass crunched under his feet with every movement. Laredo yelled a warning and snapped a couple of shots into the sunlight.

A swift look showed Kirk that the Double Lance men were moving up quietly now, many throwing caution to the wind. More guns were slamming lead at all parts around the house and he was able to hear yells and curses from the other rooms as some of the men there were hit.

'We can't hold 'em off for long,' Laredo said through tightly-clenched teeth. 'There are too many of 'em. How are we for ammunition?'

'I've about a score of shells left,' Kirk muttered. 'Make every shot count.'

Laredo grinned. 'I don't aim to do any practising',' he said. He punctuated his remark with a shot that took one of the running outlaws full in the chest, hurling him back on his feet before he swayed drunkenly and toppled over, to lie still.

The other shapes melted back into the buildings and Kirk tensed himself for the fusillade of shots which he knew would follow. He was not disappointed. Slugs crashed into the wall close to the window and he could just make out the muzzle flashes of the guns, brief stabbing flames in the dim shadows. Two men broke cover, ran forward in an attempt to throw themselves down in the thick grass that fronted the house, but they had only gone two paces before accurate fire from the house cut them down.

The volume of gunfire increased considerably over the next five minutes as the outlaws poured everything they had into the house. Kirk fired at moving shapes which were visible for only a few moments at a time before they sank down again out of sight. But each second, the men were moving closer to the building and it would not be long before they tried to smoke them out. A few well-placed brands through the bullet-smashed windows and the place would go up in flames, driving them out into the open where Culver and his men would have little difficulty in picking them off without exposing themselves to return fire.

Nearby, Laredo gave a sudden coughing grunt, slid sideways from the window, one hand going up to his shoulder. Kirk threw two swift shots at the advancing men and then moved sideways towards the other, easing him to the floor. Laredo's eyes flickered open and there was pain and dull wonder in them as he stared up at the man above him.

A spasm of pain racked through him, jerking his teeth shut as he clamped down savagely on a cry. Working quickly, Kirk ripped the shirt away from the wound. The bullet had hit high, but there was a chance it had hit the lung and he yelled loudly for Winters.

The doctor was in the room and on one knee beside the cowhand a few moments later, his face grave. He examined the bullet hole closely, then glanced up.

'How bad is he, Doc?' Kirk asked tightly. Although he

had known the old man for only a few days, he had grown to like the grizzly old cuss.

'He's tough,' said the other. 'I reckon he'll pull through. If we get the chance to tend to him properly. Those men are all around us now. There are bullets coming into the kitchen where I'm trying to tend to the others.' He let his breath go in a long sigh. 'How much longer do you think we can possibly hold out here, Brennan?'

Kirk sucked in his lips, shrugged his shoulders, ducked quickly as a volley rang out, slugs whirring across the room over their heads as they crouched down on the floor. 'Not much longer,' he admitted grimly. 'We've killed nearly a dozen of them since they tried to rush the place, but we've got precious little ammunition left. When that's done, we're finished.'

One of the men at the other window, suddenly gave a harsh yell. 'There's a bunch of riders headin' this way, Brennan!' he called. 'If they're more of Culver's men, we really are finished.'

Edging forward, keeping his head below the level of the window ledge, Kirk crawled towards the other, lifted his head cautiously until he could see through the window. Where the trail led out of town, there was a cloud of dust which clearly heralded the approach of a large bunch of men, riding hard and fast.

'That trail leads to the Double Lance spread,' said the man ominously.

Kirk nodded. He eyed the approaching men bleakly. It was impossible, at that distance, to make out who they were, but it seemed reasonably certain that once those riderless horses had arrived at the Double Lance spread, the men had been warned that something was wrong and had saddled up, riding in force into town to back up Culver.

As if to confirm this, there was a sharp shout from the

outlaws' position. Kirk recognised Culver's triumphant tone: 'You're finished now, Brennan. Those are my men riding up. Better give yourselves up while you still have the chance. I can promise you a fair trial.'

'Just like that you wanted to give me ten years ago,' Kirk called back, with derision in his tone. 'Nothin' doing, Culver.'

'All right, if that's your answer.' For a moment, Kirk thought he detected a note of thwarted anger in the other's voice. Then he swung his attention back to the riders, now moving into town, swinging in from the desert trail. He reckoned there were at least forty or fifty of them. Kirk tensed himself as the men thundered to a halt a short distance away, then began to spread out as one of the men in the lead yelled something indistinguishable at that distance.

We'll sell our lives dearly, he thought to himself; but it doesn't seem right that these men should have to die in what was really a private battle between Matt Culver and himself. His thoughts snapped off as the man beside him suddenly caught at his arm, fingers gripping it with a savage tightness.

'That's Manson out there,' he yelled in Kirk's ear. 'And there's Jeb Fallon and Clem Moody, a couple of the other ranchers.'

Kirk focused his gaze on the riders as they slid from their saddles and began moving forward on foot. For a moment he could see little because of the dust cloud which still hung around the men. Then he recognised the tall figure of Manson and a little behind, Herdson and Emmy's slight figure. Culver too, must have recognised them for he began yelling orders to his men as they laid down a volley of fire on the newcomers.

Throwing lead swiftly, to back up the others, he saw Culver's men begin to scatter now that the tables had been turned on them with a vengeance. There was no time to

wonder what had happened to the rest of the Double
Lance men back on the spread. Savage fire crashed out
from every side of the house. Kirk leapt back to his
window, reloading his gun as he went. Five men were
racing from their cover near the main street. Two toppled
on to their faces before they reached the nearest building
where Culver's men were firing frantically to cover their
retreat.

'I guess they're pullin' back,' he said thinly. 'Maybe
we'd better take the initiative. Get all of the boys together
and we'll join Herdson and the others.'

A few bullets still cut through the air as they moved out
into the open, the hot sunlight striking forcibly on their
heads and shoulders. Already, the Double Lance rannies
were scattering through the streets and alleys of the town,
bent on saving their own skins now that they were faced by
an overwhelming force. Kirk kept his eyes peeled for Matt
Culver. The other was somewhere around, he reflected,
maybe trying to escape from the town which had suddenly
become a death-trap as far as he and his men were
concerned. Firing broke out first at one spot and then
another, each burst telling him of another bunch of
Culver's men run to earth, trapped in one of the buildings. Manson's men moved here and there, and then a
shout would go up, bringing them rushing together again
and their savage firing rose into a smothering racket that
dinned at the ears.

Kirk spotted Emmy Herdson standing near the sheriff's
office and ran over to her, taking her arm and drawing her
back on to the boardwalk as desultory firing rose a short
distance away.

'Father's inside with Sheriff Cantry right now,' she said,
a trifle breathlessly. 'We got that man, Telfer, to talk. I
think Cantry is going to have to believe you now. Even if
Cantry wanted to disbelieve us, I doubt if he will when he
sees how everything is going against Matt Culver.'

WHO RIDES WITH VENGEANCE

'Have you seen Culver anywhere?'

She shook her head, the brown curls dancing on her shoulders where they escaped from the wide-brimmed hat she wore. 'Maybe the others have found him.'

'Somehow I doubt that. He wouldn't stick around when he saw that things were going against him. He'll have a plan of some kind ready and—'

He broke off sharply. There came the unmistakable sound of a solitary rider drumming along the main street from the far end of town. Peering out into the dusty street, he caught a swift glimpse of the man pushing his mount to the utmost limit. A second later, he clawed at the Colt at his waist, drawing it from its holster, but the man had ridden past him, was disappearing towards the other end of town before he could bring the weapon to bear on him.

Thrusting the gun back into leather, he leapt down into the street, ran to where some of the Manson horses were tethered. The girl shouted something from behind him as he swung up into the saddle. Turning, he called harshly: 'That was Culver. He must've got himself one of the Manson horses. I'm goin' to stop him if it's the last thing I do.'

Hauling savagely on the reins, he pulled the horse's head around, jabbed the rowels of his spurs into its flanks, sent it leaping forward. The animal responded gallantly to his urgency, flattened its ears as it headed out of town. He could just vaguely make out the faint cloud of dust, seemingly no bigger than a man's hand in the distance, which marked the position of the other rider as he spurred away from Wasatch. Culver would be heading for the Double Lance ranch, he guessed, and by taking them all by surprise in this way, he had gained a vital lead over him. He felt angry that he had not considered this possibility. The knowledge that he had taken the trouble to stampede all of the Double Lance mounts the previous night had made him overlook the fact that the Manson riders had brought horses into town with them and that inevitably, in the fighting, some of the men had been killed or injured and it had been the easiest thing in the world for Culver to grab himself a horse and light out of town as if all the devils in hell were on his trail

Bending low in the saddle, he forced the horse cruelly, feeling instinctively sorry for it, but driven to the point where he cared little for anything but the need to catch Culver and destroy him. Culver was still keeping to the twisting trail, he noticed, and it came to him that if he rode across country, he might be able to cut him off, or at least reduce the distance between them. Deliberately, he swung the horse off the trail, cut across some of the roughest country he had ever known, ground that was full of gopher holes, any one of which could snap his horse's foot if it should run into it. He could see Culver throwing quick glances over his shoulder as he rode, but already the distance was narrowing. He drew his sixgun and fired, aiming deliberately at the other's horse, but it did not go down. Probably he was still at the extreme range for this weapon. Spurring forward, he cut back towards the trail, swinging in from the right. Culver had pulled his gun, was trying to steady himself in the saddle.

Culver's face was frightened now. Sweat filmed it, shining greasily in the sunlight. He aimed another shot that passed wide, reined up for a moment and then pulled off the trail, cutting towards the low hills less than a quarter of a mile distant. Kirk fired again after the fleeing man, thought he saw the other flinch in the saddle, but it was impossible to be sure.

The other was less than fifty yards from the rugged boulders at the base of the hills when his horse suddenly hit a gopher hole and went down. Somehow, Culver managed to cling to the reins, falling clear as the horse rolled on to its side. Scrambling to his feet, Culver ran doubled-over, for cover. Kirk reined sharply, slid from the saddle on the run, darted forward, dropped sharply as Culver went down out of sight and fired at him, the bullet striking the earth within a foot of where he went down.

Sucking wind into his lungs, he lay quite still behind the upthrusting rock which afforded him a little protection, filled the empty chambers of his gun from his belt. He studied the terrain ahead of him thoughtfully. He was slightly lower down than Culver's position and beyond the rocks where the other lay was a wide stretch of open ground. Now we'll see just how good he is, Kirk thought grimly to himself as he lay there on his stomach. We'll see if his nerves are good enough to give him the patience to wait things out.

Time passed slowly. For a long while, there was neither sound nor movement near the rock where Matt Culver lay hidden. Then the other's voice lifted into the clinging, uneasy stillness.

'Listen, Brennan. I know you're out there, and I know why you want to kill me. But there ain't no point in both of us shooting up the other just for the sake of a ten-year-old misunderstanding. I knew as soon as you'd pulled out that I was wrong, that you were innocent of the rustlin' charge, or the murder of that man on the trail. I can square everythin' for you with Cantry. He'll do exactly as I say. I know how you feel about Emmy Herdson. Well, there ain't no reason I can see why you two shouldn't get hitched and have a ranch of your own.'

'Save your breath with all of these promises,' Kirk called back. 'I swore ten years ago that I'd come back and kill you. I mean to do just that. As for the Double Lance spread, I figure that Herdson will be takin' it over again soon as the legal owner. You've got nothin' now – nothin' at all.'

'Damn you, Brennan. We could have been the two most important and wealthy men in the whole goddamned territory. Why throw all of that away just to get even with me?'

'That's probably somethin' you'd never understand,' Kirk said ominously. 'Now if you've finished speakin' your piece, just stand up and face me like a man. You'll get an even chance which is more than you gave me ten years ago.'

The other made no answer and stillness settled over the rocks again. Kirk glanced sideways, noticed the shallow depression in the ground that ran from where he lay to a point some twenty feet to his right. It was worth a try. Squirming forward, he wriggled snake-like into the depression, moving with strong heaves of his arms and shoulders. Every second he expected to feel the terrible impact of a slug in his body but his luck was holding and it was evident that the other could not see him from where he lay.

At the end of the depression, he paused, raised his head cautiously. He could just make out Culver's figure lying prone behind the rock with the harsh glare of the sunlight picking him out starkly. He could have drilled him there and then, but it was not in him to drop a man like that.

'Hold it right there, Culver!' he yelled.

He saw the other freeze at the sound of his voice, stiffening in every limb. Then, slowly, the other turned his head. There was an expression of intense surprise written on his face. He still held his Colt in his right hand but he made no attempt to lift it or use it.

'Drop the gun, or use it,' Kirk said harshly.

'Listen, Brennan. Like I said, we can both be big men in the territory. It's large enough for both of us and—'

He propped himself abruptly on his elbow, jerked up the gun, face twisted into a  harsh grimace of hatred and anger. Kirk saw the other's eyes narrowed in the second before he squeezed off a single shot, the Colt hammering against his wrist. Close on the explosion, he heard the other fire, but the bullet went wide as Culver slumped

159

forward on to his face his hat, falling off his head. His hair ruffled a little in the breeze as Kirk got to his feet and walked carefully over, standing above the other, the barrel of his gun lined on the man's back, but he made no move.

Whistling up his mount, he lifted the limp body over the saddle, turned and began walking the horse back to the trail. The sun scorched his shoulders through his shirt but there was a strange sense of peace in his mind. For the first time, in ten years, he felt relaxed and at peace with himself. It had been a long and rough trail he had been forced to ride but the man who had been the cause of it all, now lay dead over his saddle, arms and legs hanging limply, head lolling stupidly near the horse's belly.

As he neared Wasatch, he spotted the group of horsemen riding towards him. They reined up as they reached him and Herdson leaned forward in his saddle, staring down at Culver's body. His face was grim, but his tone even as he said: 'I see you caught him, Kirk. His empire was finished anyway. I think he must have known that when he rode out.'

'Maybe he was tryin' to get back to the ranch and bring up the rest of his boys.'

'Wouldn't have done him any good,' affirmed the other. 'We took care of them on our way into town. Those who weren't killed will be halfway to the border by now.'

Kirk nodded wearily. It was as if a tremendous weight had been suddenly lifted from his mind. He turned his head at the drumming of hoofs, saw Emmy riding towards him along the trail and stepped forward to meet her, everything else forgotten.